D0899126

Book Three:
Meerm

F. Paul Wilson

This special signed edition is
limited to 750 numbered copies.

This is number 84.

Book Three:

Meerm

Book Three:

Meerm

F. Paul Wilson

CEMETERY DANCE PUBLICATIONS

Baltimore

❖ 2002 ❖

Signed Hardcover Edition ISBN 1-58767-050-X

Manufactured in the United States of America.

FIRST EDITION

Cemetery Dance Publications
P.O. Box 943
Abingdon, Maryland 21009
E-mail: cdancepub@aol.com

www.cemeterydance.com

For Dave Auerbach:
genetics maven and
fellow Jill Sobule fan

1

The Bronx

Poor Meerm. Poor, poor Meerm. She ver sick sim. Meerm nev sick before. Not like be sick. Food come up sometime stead go down. And tummy hurt. Hurt-hurt-hurt. Bad tummy hurt all time.

But sick not bad all time. Sick Meerm get own room, room all by self stead of down big room with all other sim. Sick room have nice bed and own bathroom, all for Meerm. Not need share. But Meerm little room still have metal bar window like sim big room downstair. Sick Meerm also get good food, special food, come on own plate. Meerm not have get self from pot like down in sim big room. Sick room food better. Yum-yum. Meerm wish she not such sick sim so she like food more. Sick Meerm not hungry sim like well Meerm.

Meerm lonely here sometime in sick room but Meerm not downstair where mans and lady stick sharp thing in sim, sometime take blood. Take-take-take. And man with hair face do very bad hurt thing to Meerm and other sim. But not here sick room. No sharp stick here. No one hurt Meerm sick room.

Sick room top floor. Meerm like look window at light on street down below. Meerm wish—

What that? Loud noise from downstair. Again! Loud noise again. *Crack!* Like giant plate break. Meerm go door, open just little and listen. Hear loud fear word by mans and lady, hear new man voice shout more loud, hear sim voice, many voice cry ee-ee-ee! Ver fraid, other sim.

Now Meerm hear new man voice shout, "Where is she?" and hear ver fraid lady say, "Upstairs! We moved her upstairs!"

Meerm ver fraid. Make belly hurt badder. Hear many loud feet come stair. Meerm want close sick room door but no good. Across hall see ladder up wall. Ladder up to little door. Meerm sure locked—all door here locked—but Meerm try. Must try. Too fraid stay sick room.

Meerm jump cross hall, climb ladder, push little door. Move! Door move! Meerm so happy. Climb up roof. Close little door. Meerm listen. Hear new man voice shout. Ver, ver mad. Hear foot on ladder. Come roof! What Meerm do? Where go?

There. Metal hole. Meerm can fit? Run and crawl in. Squeeze ver hard. Sink inside just as mans come roof. Meerm close eye, not breathe as mans run all round roof. Man look in metal hole but not see Meerm.

Mans ver mad as leave roof. Meerm safe but still not move. Wait. Meerm will wait long long time. Wait until—

What smell? Smoke! Smoke and hot come up vent. Meerm get out and stand on roof. Tar hot on foot. Smoke all round. Meerm ver ver scare. Run round roof, see fire evwhere. Look down. Flame all round, come out bar on all window. Meerm not want die. But roof ver hot. Tar melt under Meerm foot. What Meerm do?

Meerm scream. No one hear. No one near.

2

Manhattan

Patrick stood at his hotel window and gazed down at the top of Madison Square Garden and the giant Christmas snowman atop its entrance. The unrisen December sun was just beginning to lighten the low clouds lidding the city, but Patrick had been awake for hours.

This had been the pattern every night since the poisoning of the sims. Fall asleep easily—with the help of a couple of stiff Scotches—and then find himself wide awake at three A.M. or so with his mind sifting through the litterbox his life had become the past few months.

All because of an argument in a country club men's room. That was where it had started. But what if he hadn't chosen that moment to go to the bathroom? What if he'd waited until after that second drink? Someone else might have been in there instead of Carter, and with another person present, Tome wouldn't have asked him to unionize the club sims. Patrick would have gone in, emptied his bladder, and walked out. And if that had happened, where would he be now?

For one thing, he'd still have a law practice; he'd also have a house instead of a fire-blackened foundation; and he'd even have a love life, such as it had been.

Probably wouldn't have spent Thanksgiving alone, either. Ever since his folks retired to South Carolina, they'd always called and insisted he come down for Thanksgiving. Not this year. That was Dad's doing, Patrick was sure.

A steamfitter and diehard union man all his life, his father had been so proud when Patrick became the first member of the family to graduate college. But he hadn't been so crazy about Patrick's idea of going to law school. He couldn't afford to send him, and probably wouldn't have if he could. So Patrick had paid his own way. If he'd become a crusader for the labor movement, Dad might have bragged about his son the lawyer; but Patrick had joined the lumpen proletariat of the profession: not a crook, not a shyster, just another of that vast slick crew using the letter of a law to circumvent its spirit. But Dad had been able to live with that.

Apparently Dad was not able to handle the idea of his son starting a union for sims. He'd called once and vented his feelings. Patrick had sympathized but backing down had been out of the question then. He hadn't realized just how upset his father was until Thanksgiving had come and gone without an invitation.

And so here he was: jobless, homeless, alone, and functionally orphaned. He'd survived an attempt on his life, but his only clients—non-humans, to boot—hadn't been so lucky. And along the way he'd become a notorious figure, admired by few, reviled by many. On the plus side he'd become involved—not romantically, but he hoped that would change—with the most intriguing, dynamic, fascinating woman he'd ever met. That in turn had led to a masked mystery man who'd invited him to join a nameless fifth column movement to bring down one of the world's most powerful multinational corporations.

"And I said yes," he whispered, still not believing it.

This is not me, he kept telling himself. This is somebody else. All I wanted out of life was stability and a few bucks. Okay, stability and many, many bucks. That was why I went into law. I am not a risk taker. I am not an adrenaline junky. How did I come to this? And how do I get out of it?

Easy. Just say no. Pack up and walk away.

And do what? Labor relations? After what he'd been through, could he go back to sitting at a table and listening to union and management argue over the length of coffee breaks or who qualified for daycare? Not likely. Though he'd been burned out of his home and run off the road, these past few months had been the best of his life.

So for the foreseeable future he'd stick this out and see where it took him.

Hopefully it would soon take him out of this hotel. Zero had suggested he relocate himself and his practice to Manhattan. Romy had laughed off his suggestion that he move in with her while he hunted for an office and an apartment. So for the time being, home was a room in the Hotel Pennsylvania. Finding space—whether living or office—wasn't easy. The prices in Manhattan were up in the Mir's old spot.

The jangle of the phone startled him. He stepped through the dark room to the night table, found the phone, and fumbled the receiver to his ear.

Romy's voice: "Am I interrupting something?"

"Only my daily predawn reverie."

She gave him an address. "If you haven't anything better to do, meet me there ASAP. I'll wait for you."

Patrick sensed strain in her voice, but before he could ask any details she hung up.

Dutifully he pulled on yesterday's clothes, grabbed a large container of coffee on his way through the lobby, and ventured into the early morning December chill of Seventh Avenue in search of a taxi.

The driver shot him a look when he read off the address. "You're sure?"

"I'm sure," Patrick told him after double checking.

The driver shrugged—reluctantly, Patrick thought—and gunned the cab into the traffic.

Patrick considered that look and thought, Romy, Romy, what are you getting me into now?

3

The Bronx

All too soon Patrick understood the driver's reaction. The address was in the fabled borough of the Bronx. Not the nice Botanical Gardens Bronx, but the bad Bronx, the *Bonfire of the Vanities* / "Fort Apache" Bronx. This particular section embodied most people's worst expectations: a wasteland of scattered buildings, some occupied, some abandoned, all battered, interspersed with vacant, garbage-strewn lots.

"Christ, what happened here?" Patrick muttered as he stepped out of the cab.

As soon as he closed the door behind him the taxi chirped its tires and zoomed away. Patrick couldn't blame him. At least there were lots of cops around. No need to ask why they were here: the charred, smoking ruin of what must have been a cousin to the neighboring derelict buildings was the obvious center of attention. No fire trucks in sight now, but a couple of red SUVs bearing fire department logos stood out among the cluster of blue-and-white units blocking the street.

He glanced around and spotted Romy's long black leather coat among the blue uniforms. She was standing outside the yellow tape and turned as he approached.

"Good," she said, but no smile lit her grim expression. "You're here. We can get started."

" 'How are you, Patrick?' " he said. " 'Did you sleep well?' Why, yes, Romy. Thank you for asking. And how was your night?"

"Save it," she said, lifting the tape and ducking under. "Follow me."

Patrick complied as she approached a burly, clipboard-wielding sergeant.

"Excuse me, Sergeant," she said, holding up a leather ID folder. "Romy Cadman, OPRR. Please fill me in on what you've found."

The sergeant swiveled his head and gave her a quick up and down with his pale blue eyes.

"O-P-*what*?"

"Office for the Protection of Research Risks. We're federal. We monitor labs and test subjects, animal and human. Lieutenant Milancewich at Manhattan South notified me that this building might have housed an unlicensed lab and that sims could have been involved."

Patrick knew Romy had no authority to be here: sims did not fall under OPRR's aegis. She was here for Zero and the organization, and for herself as well. But he said nothing, just stood by and admired her moxie as she weathered the sergeant's hostile stare.

"He did, did he? Well, I ain't heard of no OPRR and no Lieutenant Milancewich, and you're one hell of a long way from Manhattan South. We can handle this just fine without no feds nosing into it."

"Of course you can," Romy said. "OPRR has no investigative authority. We're only offering help. We know labs. We can trace diagnostic equipment better and faster than anyone. We know lab animals. If sims were used as test subjects here, we can help you track them. Our interest is purely statistical: we're keeping tally of illegal labs and what biologicals they produce." She opened her leather coat to return her ID folder to an inner pocket, revealing in the process a tight, black, ribbed knit sweater and long legs slinking from a short black skirt. "We're a resource, sergeant. Use us."

The sergeant's eyes lingered on her coat as she tied it closed with a leather belt, then he stuck out his hand.

"Andy Yarger."

Romy smiled and shook his hand. "Call me Romy."

Patrick resisted the natural impulse to close his eyes and shake his head. If that had been him popping up in front of Sergeant Yarger with an OPRR ID, he'd have been kicked back on the far side of the yellow tape before he'd spoken word one. But Romy had just reduced this Bronx-hardened cop to a lap dog.

The weaker sex? Yeah, tell me about it.

"And who's this?" Yarger said, jutting his chin Patrick's way.

"That's my assistant, Patrick."

"That's me, all right. Faithful sidekick and gofer."

Yarger narrowed his eyes. "Ain't I seen you before?"

"About the lab equipment?" Romy prompted.

"Your lieutenant friend was right. We found bits and pieces of all sorts of lab equipment in the wreckage. Some of it's been identified as—lemme see." He consulted his clipboard. "Here we go: hematology machines, blood chemistry analyzers, immu...immuno..."

Romy was nodding. "I get the picture. Who identified the equipment?"

"Couple of the M-E's boys."

"M-E?" Patrick said when he saw Romy's stricken look. "Sims were killed?"

"We should be so lucky. Nah. Just one very dead, very crisp human corpse. Male, age unknown."

Patrick stared at the burned-out ruins and couldn't help grimacing. They reminded him of what remained of his house, and how "crisp" he could have been.

"What a way to go."

"Wasn't the fire that got him. A bullet saved him from that."

"Really?" Patrick said. "You're sure?"

Yarger gave him a steely look.

"What he means," Romy added quickly, "is how can you tell if he was, as you say, 'very crisp'?"

The sergeant poked an index finger against the center of his forehead. "Ain't never seen no fire burn a little hole here and blow off the back of a skull, know what I'm saying?"

"I hear you," Romy said. "But no, er, 'crisp' sims?"

"Not yet anyways. Don't expect to find none either."

"But Lieutenant Milancewich mentioned sims."

"Right. Witnesses saw armed men herding a bunch of sims and some humans into a couple of vans just before the place went up." He shook his head. "I don't know what sort of incendiary devices they used, but they musta been beauts. Place went up like it was made of paper."

"But there *could* be dead sims in there," Romy persisted.

Yarger crooked a finger and started moving away. "C'mere. I'll show you why there won't be."

Patrick and Romy followed him to a taped-off area near the corner. Yarger stopped and pointed to the sidewalk.

"That's why."

Red spray-painted letters spread across the pavement.

FREE THE SIMS!
DEATH TO SIM OPPRESSORS!
SLA

"SLA?" Patrick said with a glance at Romy.

Her face was troubled when she met his eyes. "I know what you're thinking," she whispered. "But no. Impossible. He'd never."

"The Symbionese Liberation Army?" Patrick raised his voice to cover hers. "Didn't they kidnap Patty Hearst?"

"Different group," Yarger said. "These assholes are the '*Sim* Liberation Army.' Don't that beat all."

"How do you know?" Romy said.

"That's what they called themselves in the note they left."

"What else did it say?"

"Buncha sim-hugger garbage. The usual stuff. You know the rap."

"May I see it?"

Yarger gave Romy a you-gotta-be-kidding look. "Forensics got it." He turned as someone called his name. "Yeah. Be right there." Then back to Romy. "Look, you wanna leave me your card, we'll call you if we think we need help. But don't wait up for it. And for the time being, stay on the other side of the tape, okay?"

Patrick expected Romy to press him further, but she simply nodded. Patrick lifted the tape for her and she ducked under. She pulled out a compact camera and began snapping pictures.

"For your scrapbook?"

"For Zero. He'll want to see."

"Speaking of Zero," he said, leaning close and whispering. "Did you call him about this?"

"You don't call Zero. You leave a message."

"Could he be behind this?"

She lowered her camera. Her look was fierce. "I told you—"

"Does he consult you on everything he does? Of course not. So how do you know?"

She started snapping pictures again.

"I just do. He lets me take care of the brothels and places like this. That's *my* job."

"Well just what sort of place is it—or I guess I should say, *was* it?"

"A globulin farm."

"A what?"

"It's—wait. Did you see that Asian man over there?"

"No. Where?"

"I just pointed the camera in his direction and he ducked away. Where did he go?"

INE DO NO
LICE LINE DO
FREE THE SI
EATH TO SIM OPP
SLA

She rose on tiptoe to scan the area, then quickly ducked back.

"Oh, hell!" She spun, turning her back to Patrick as she started moving. "Don't look around, just follow me."

"Why?"

"Just do it. I don't want to—"

"Well, well!" said a man's voice behind him. "If it isn't Ms. Romy Cadman of OPRR. Fancy meeting you here."

"Shit!" Romy hissed; it sounded more like escaping steam than a word.

As she turned, so did he. He saw a swarthy, broad-shouldered man in an overcoat swaggering toward them. Patrick took an instant dislike to his smug expression. But his cold, dark eyes were his most arresting feature. Patrick felt like a mouse being scrutinized by a rattlesnake. But then the man's gaze flicked away. Patrick had been demoted from lunch to background scenery.

"Mr. Portero," Romy said in a deep-freeze voice. "What a surprise."

"I don't see why it should be. Sims were reported on the scene, and SimGen has a vital interest in the welfare of all sims."

"Sure it does," Romy said, drawing out the first word. "But to send its chief of security?"

" 'Free the sims' is not a phrase SimGen takes lightly, especially when it involves murder. I decided to look into this myself."

"You should introduce yourself to that sergeant over there," Romy said. "His name's Yarger and he's anxious for all the help he can get."

"I'm sure he is." Portero jerked a thumb toward the smoking ruin. "What do you think? Globulin farm?"

"That's my guess."

"Could someone explain that to me? What's a globulin farm?"

The man turned his glittering stare on Patrick. "And you are . . .?"

"This is a friend," Romy said. "Patrick Sullivan. Patrick, meet Mr. Portero, security chief at SimGen."

"Oh, yes," Portero said. "I believe I've heard of you. Some sort of lawyer, right?"

Patrick noticed that Portero had clasped his hands behind his back as he spoke. A handshake seemed out of the question, so Patrick didn't offer one.

"Some sort, yes," Patrick said. "But about this globulin farm . . . ?"

Romy said, "When you get sick, when a virus or bacterium invades your body, you fight back through your immune system. It forms proteins, immune globulins known as antibodies, to kill the invaders. That's called active immunity. But let's say you jab yourself with a needle that's infected with, say, hepatitis B or C. You could ward off infection by either of those viruses through passive immunity—by being injected with antibodies from someone already immune to those infections."

Patrick was getting the picture. A few months ago he'd have had to ask another half dozen questions to fill in the blanks, but during that time he'd been exposed to enough mistreatment of sims to allow him to do the filling himself.

"I get it. Since sims are so close to humans, some slimeball gets the bright idea of kidnapping or hijacking a group and infecting them with viruses and selling off the immunity of whichever ones survive."

"Exactly," Romy said. "And sometimes if a sim survives one virus, they infect it with another, and then another, until they can harvest a multi-immune globulin. The more diseases covered, the higher the price per dose."

"Ain't science grand," Patrick said.

"But it's not a one-time thing. A sim will produce those antibodies for as long as it lives. All the farmers have to do is keep it alive and healthy and they've got themselves a cash cow they can literally milk for years."

"A globulin farm." He stared at the blackened ruins. "Not anymore."

"Thanks to this so-called SLA," Portero said. He stared at Romy. "Ever hear of them, Romy?"

Patrick felt his insides clench at the sound of her first name on Portero's lizard lips, but said nothing.

Romy regarded him coolly. "Not till this morning."

"I don't understand their methods," Portero said, rubbing his jaw as he looked around. "I can see them making off with the sims, to free them later. But why fire the building? What if they'd missed a few sims in their raid? They'd have been cooked just like that corpse." He turned to Romy. "Did your sergeant friend mention finding any sim bodies?"

"No, thank God."

"Yes . . . thank God." Portero's eyes became distant; he seemed to recede for a moment, then gathered himself. "But why did these terrorists make off with the humans as well?"

"Your guess is as good as mine," Romy said.

Portero smiled as he shook his head. "Oh, I doubt that, Romy. I doubt that very much."

And then he swaggered away.

"Something about this has got him worried," Romy said. "He's putting on a good show, but something's bothering him."

"Is that why he never blinks?"

"He doesn't have to; he has nictating membranes."

"That figures. And his tiny reptile heart is set on you."

Romy's lips twisted. "Yeah, I know."

"But I'm taller."

She smiled for the first time since he'd arrived. "You know, sometimes I'm glad you're around."

"Only sometimes?"

She hooked her arm through his and started walking. "Let's go grab some breakfast and wait for Zero to beep me."

"Excellent idea, but in a better neighborhood, if you please."

As they moved away he glanced back at Portero, intending to give him a look-what-I've-got wink, but thought better of it when he saw the fierce look in those icy dark eyes.

4

Manhattan

Romy's beeper didn't buzz until almost noon. She checked the readout:

garage 1pm Ø

She was glad for the change from the Worth Street basement. Use one place too often and eventually the wrong person was going to make the right connection. She and Patrick hopped a cab to the West Side.

"I don't see a garage," Patrick said as they stepped out onto Ninth Avenue in the Thirties.

"It's down the street, closer to Tenth. But let's stand here awhile. Just to be sure no one followed us."

The sun had poked through the clouds but did little to moderate the chill wind whistling through the concrete canyons.

"Do you ever ask yourself if you're crazy?" Patrick said, looking around as if expecting to see trench-coated men lurking in doorways.

"All the time."

"Good. That's a healthy sign. Because I think we're both crazy."

"I think I know where this is going."

"Do you? Great. Then maybe you can tell me why we're at the beck and call of this guy. Who is he? What's driving him? Why's he doing this? What's in it for him?"

Romy had sought the answers to those questions herself, and had done her damnedest to pierce Zero's veil of secrecy. She knew from glimpses of skin at his throat and between his gloves and cuffs that he was a white male, so she'd tried working up a list of pale males who had sufficient assets to fund such a far-flung organization, eliminating those whose interests conflicted with Zero's. It proved a futile exercise. After years of trying she was no closer to the truth now than when she'd started.

"I can't answer all your questions," she told Patrick, "but I can tell you why he's doing it: To stop the slave trade of sentient beings."

"But what's in it for him?"

"Cessation of the slave trade of sentient beings."

"Bull. Idealistic crap."

The words stung Romy. "You don't believe people can be motivated by ideals?"

"Foot soldiers can be, and they often are. But not the generals, not the guys running the war. They've got something else driving them, whether it's a better place in history or a spot closer to their god or riches or fame or glory or power or revenge or guilt; there's always something in it for them."

"What about Gandhi? Schindler? Father Damien? Mother Teresa?"

He shrugged. "Everyone in the world knows their names. Maybe that's what they were after."

"I'm glad I'm not you," she said. "What an awful way to view life."

"Maybe I've seen too many so-called idealists caught with their hands in the till."

"A corrupt individual doesn't corrupt the ideal." How could she explain this? "There's an obscure Paul Simon song called "Everything Put Together Falls Apart." It doesn't get played much but—"

"I remember it. A jazzy, bluesy thing."

"That's it. I don't recall the lyrics but I've never forgotten the title, because I've always added my own coda: *Unless you act.* The world does not become a better place and *stay* a better place on its own. It takes effort. Constant effort, because entropy is the default process. And so every day is a battle against the tendency for things to devolve to a lower state—of existence, of civilization, of meaning, of everything that matters. That's why I'm with Zero. Because everything put together falls apart—unless you act."

"But I can't see sims as entropic. If anything—"

"To create a new self-aware species is a magnificent accomplishment; to use them as slaves is to drag that accomplishment through the mud; to accept that circumstance is poison for the human soul."

"No argument there, and I didn't bring this up to start one. But look at the situation. Here's a guy who's spent a fortune—we're talking millions—setting up this nameless organization to stop SimGen, and then he hides his identity from everyone who works for him. I can see him not trusting me, but what about you? You've worked with him for years. He's got to know you're in this for the long run. Why doesn't he let you see his face?"

"How do you know he hasn't?" she shot back.

Patrick's eyebrows jumped. "Has he?"

"No."

"See what I mean?"

"Maybe he's someone we'd recognize."

"Yeah, there's a thought. You know . . . he seems to be built a lot like David Letterman."

Romy wasn't going to dignify that with an answer.

"Let's walk," she said, satisfied that no one was on their tail.

"Seriously, though, I'd feel a lot better about this Zero guy if I knew what makes his motor run." Patrick seemed to be in summation mode as they headed toward Tenth Avenue, walking sideways, the wind ruffling his blond hair as he gestured with his hands. "If it's because a SimGen truck ran over his mother when he was a kid, fine. Or if he's got huge short positions of SimGen stock, fine. Or even if it's because of something crazy like Mercer Sinclair stole his girlfriend in seventh grade, I don't care. I just want to know so I can have a handle on how much he'll risk to get what he wants. Because so far we're the ones in the line of fire, not him. He wasn't in my car when it was run off the Saw Mill. He wasn't at Beacon Ridge when the sims offered to share their poisoned food with us."

Romy hated to admit it, but Patrick was making sense. She'd been taken with Zero from their first meeting. She'd sensed the fire burning beneath all his layers of disguise, and she'd been warmed by its heat. But what fueled that fire? It was a question she'd never asked.

She'd assumed it burned the same as her own, an all-consuming desire to right a wrong. Was that a foolish assumption? Perhaps. But she had to go with what she knew.

"All I can tell you," she said, "is that I believe in his cause and he's never let me down. I don't intend to let him down."

He sighed. "Fair enough. I'm trusting your judgment. For now."

Down near Tenth, Romy stopped before a white doorway next to an equally white roll-up garage door and pressed a buzzer. She glanced up into the eye of an overhead security camera and nodded once, signaling that all was clear. The door buzzed open.

Inside, a single dusty bulb glowed in the ceiling. They found Zero, barely visible in the gloom, his tall lean figure swathed in sweater, jeans, ski mask, dark glasses, and gloves, pacing beside a beat-up Ford Econoline delivery van, once white, now soot gray.

"Have you heard any more about this SLA group?" he said without preamble.

Romy sensed the tension in his voice.

"Nothing. I called a few of the cops I know but nothing's broken yet beyond the identity of the corpse found in the ashes: his name was Craig Strickland, a twenty-four-year old with a history of assaults."

"Doesn't sound like your typical globulin farmer."

"They figure he was security. He may have tried to resist. As for the SLA, an all-points has been issued but they and their captives seem to have vanished."

"Two vans filled with human and sim hostages and no one's seen a thing?"

"Not yet."

Zero slammed a gloved fist against the already dented side of the van. "Damn! Who *are* these psychos? What do they hope to accomplish for sims by murdering humans? Not that the world is any poorer for the loss of a globulin farmer, but killing him shifts focus in the wrong direction. Everyone's attention is on the murder now rather than the sims the dead man was abusing."

"Pardon my paranoia," Patrick said, "but maybe that's the whole point. Maybe these aren't sim sympathizers. Maybe SimGen is behind them."

"All right," Zero said. "I don't buy that, but let's assume SimGen has somehow come to the conclusion that the gains from high-profile murder will, by some stretch of the imagination, outweigh the risks. If that's true, and if they're going to spray paint 'Death to sim oppressors' at the crime scene, then why kill only one of the globulin farmers? Why not make a real statement and kill them all? Why spirit them away along with the sims?"

"Hostages?"

Zero's expression was unreadable behind his mask and shades, but Romy could imagine a dour look as he stopped his pacing and faced Patrick.

"Let's try to imagine how many people would step forward to pay a globulin farmer's ransom."

Patrick shrugged. "Okay. So much for the hostage idea."

" 'Death to sim oppressors!' " Zero said, slamming his fist against the van again. "Damn them! Idiots!"

Romy had never seen him show so much emotion. She found it oddly exciting.

Down, girl, she told herself as she pulled her digital camera's diskette from her pocket.

She said, "I may have another piece to add to the puzzle. I took a shot of an Asian man—Japanese, I think—at the scene. He ducked away as soon as he saw the camera. I've never seen him before, and it may mean nothing, but he was definitely camera shy."

Zero seemed to have calmed himself. He took the diskette. "I'll see if he's anyone we should know about."

"But what's the plan?" she said. "What do we do about this SLA?"

"I can't see that we have any choice but to wait and see. I doubt we'll have much of a wait. A group like that won't want to stay out of the headlines long. But in the meantime we won't be idle. We're ready to make our move against Manassas Ventures."

Romy stiffened. "When?"

"Tomorrow morning. Are you up for it?"

"I think so."

She wasn't looking forward to this. It involved playing a role, pretending she was a kind of person she despised. She hoped she could bring it off.

Zero's dark lenses were trained on her. "Something wrong?"

She didn't want to let him in on her apprehensions. He had enough on his plate.

"I just keep thinking about those sims," and that was no lie. "Whoever these SLA people are, I hope they're taking good care of them."

"Amen to that," Zero muttered. He shook his head. "'Free the sims.' Don't they understand? Sims have never been allowed to learn to fend for themselves. A free sim isn't free at all. It's a lost soul."

5

The Bronx

Poor Meerm.

Meerm feel so bad. So more bad than last night. Now Meerm still belly-sick but cold and hungry also too. Also too arm hurt where burn while climb down building side. And leg hurt from fall ground. Hurt-hurt-hurt. Meerm hurt all over.

And Meerm ver fraid. Hide in bottom old empty building. No window and many rat. Rat sniff at Meerm burn. Shoo way, throw rock. Bad place this. And so cold. Meerm miss sick room and yum-yum sick food. Wish go back but sick room gone. She go look in dark. All burn, all gone.

Meerm ver lonely. Meerm ver fraid. Not know what do. Not know where go.

6

Hicksville, Long Island

Shortly after eight A.M. Romy stepped through the front door of the small two-story office building and made a show of looking at the directory. The vestibule was clean but showing some wear around the edges. Just like the building, which was a good thirty years old and typical of the boxy, clapboard style popular back in the seventies. The tenants listed—a dentist, a real estate office, an insurance agent—were typical of any suburban office building; all except the lessee of the small corner office on the second floor: a venture capital company worth billions.

Romy hurried up to the second floor and found the door to Suite 2-C. A strictly no-frills black plastic plaque spelled out MANASSAS VENTURES, INC in small white letters. She waited outside the door until she heard someone climbing the steps, then she started knocking.

A woman in a colorful smock appeared, heading for the dental office, and Romy turned to her.

"When does the Manassas Ventures staff usually arrive?"

The woman looked dumbfounded. "You know, I don't think I've ever seen anybody coming or going from that office."

That's because no one does, Romy thought. Zero had had the place under observation for weeks.

"Really?" Romy said, putting her hand on the doorknob and rattling it. "I've been trying to reach them by phone but no one returns my messages, so I thought I'd come over in person and—"

The door swung inward.

"Now isn't that something," the dental assistant said as she stepped forward for a peek at the interior. "They must've forgot to lock it."

Morning sunlight streamed through the sheer curtains behind an empty receptionist's desk and flared the dust motes dancing through the air. No shortage of dust here—the desktop sported a good eighth of an inch.

"Hello?" Romy said, stepping inside. The air smelled stale, musty. No one had opened a window for a long, long time. "Anybody home?"

"Good luck," the woman told Romy and started back toward her office.

"Thanks."

Romy had to act quickly. She glanced up, searching for the strand of monofilament she'd been told she'd find hanging from the central light fixture. There it was, a length of fine fishing line, barely visible.

Two of Zero's people had broken in over the weekend. They'd unlatched the door and rigged the fixture to drop when the fishing line was pulled.

The original plan had been to loosen the hinges on the door so that it would fall outward when Romy tugged on it. She would let it knock her down and claim a terrible back injury. But Patrick had vetoed the idea, saying an injury caused by the door to the suite might leave the landlord as the liable party rather than the tenant. And it was the tenant they were after.

The most open-and-shut scenario—he'd called it *res ipso loquitor*—was to arrange for Romy to be "injured" by a tenant-installed fixture. After some quick reconnoitering, the fluorescent box in the ceiling over the reception area received the nod.

Romy was supposed to pull the string and let it crash to the floor, then stagger out and collapse in the hall, pretending it had landed on her.

Pretend . . . she'd never been good at pretending. How was she supposed to slump to the floor out there and moan and groan about being hurt and have anyone buy it? And the Manassas people, when they heard about it they'd know that what happened here was all a sham, a set-up designed to drag them into the legal system and expose their corporate innards. They'd respond by deploying their lawyers to use every possible legal ploy to keep their secrets under wraps.

They'll play hide, we'll play seek. A game.

But this was not a game to her. Romy was serious about this. She'd show them just how serious.

Acting quickly, before the dental assistant could reach her office across the hall, Romy stepped under the fixture and yanked on the line.

Her scream of pain was real.

7

Patrick sat in the driver seat of Zero's van, idly watching the office building that housed Manassas Ventures. He'd parked across the street in a church parking lot—Our Lady of Something-or-other—and left the engine idling to run the heater, but he was keeping his window open to let out the pungent odor that seemed to be ingrained into the van's metal frame. The driver seat seemed little more than a sheet of newspaper spread over a collection of rusty springs.

But the sharp jabs against his butt were inconsequential compared to the discomfort of sharing the van with the shadowy form seated behind him. Here was a perfect opportunity to probe Zero, maybe get a line on what made this bird tick, but Patrick found himself tongue tied.

What do you say to a masked man?

Had to give it a shot: "Do you mind if I ask you a personal question?"

Zero's deep voice echoed from the dark recess at the rear of the van. "Depends."

"Why you call yourself 'Zero'?"

"That is my name."

Ooookay. Try another tack. "How about them Mets?" That was usually a foolproof conversation opener, especially out here on the Island, even in the off season. "What do you think of that last round of trades?"

"I don't follow sports."

Okay, strike that topic. Maybe if we concentrate more on the moment . . .

"You have any idea what this van was used for before you got it?"

"It was a delivery truck run by a Korean Christian group in Yonkers."

"Smells like they spilled a gallon of roast puppy stew on the way to the annual church potluck dinner."

Patrick heard a soft chuckle. "I can think of worse things to spill."

Hey, he laughs!

"You mean, be grateful for small favors, right?"

"Small and large. I'm grateful the Reverend Eckert has finally been able to purchase space on a satellite."

"That means he'll be beaming his anti-SimGen sermons direct."

"Right. No more worries about SimGen influencing the syndicate that's been carrying him. Not only can he beam his shows to the syndicate, but he's now got access to anyone with a satellite dish."

"Nice. A big jump in audience."

"I'm grateful too," Zero said, "for how well you and Romy are working together."

"So far, so good. She's a piece of work."

"That she is. One very intense young woman. Tell me, Patrick, do you hope for a closer relationship between the two of you?"

Odd question. "Do you mean working or personal?"

"Personal."

"Is there something I don't know?" Patrick said, turning to look at him. He wished he'd take off that mask. "Is there something going on between you and Romy? Because if there is—"

Zero gave a dismissive wave. "Nothing, I assure you. I am . . . unavailable."

That was a relief.

"Well, okay, but all I can say is, whether or not we go to the next step is entirely up to her. If you're worried about a romance between us interfering with our job performance, rest easy. The lady has thus far found the strength of character to resist my charms."

"Which I'm sure are considerable."

"'From yer lips to Gawd's ear', as me grandmother used to say."

"Speaking of God, I've been looking at this church. Are you Catholic?"

"With a name like Patrick Michael Sullivan, could I be anything else?"

"Are you a practicing Catholic?"

"No. Pretty much the fallen-away variety. Haven't seen the inside of a church for some time."

"But you do believe in God."

"Yeah, sure." Where was this going?

"Did you know that some sims believe in God, even pray to Him?"

"No. I didn't." For some reason the idea made him uncomfortable. "Any particular faith?"

"They tend toward Catholicism. They like all the statues, although they find the crucifix disturbing. They're most comfortable with the Virgin Mary. Pick through any sim barrack and you'll usually find a few statues of her."

"I can see that. A mother figure is comforting."

"Sims pray to God, Patrick. But does God hear them?"

"What do you mean?"

"Do sims have souls?"

"This is heavy stuff."

"Most enlightened believers accept evolution. Genetics makes it impossible for an intelligent person to deny a common ancestor between chimps and humans. Some theologians posit a 'transcendental intervention' along the evolutionary tree, the moment when God imbued an early human with a soul. So I ask you Patrick: when human genes were spliced into chimps to make sims, did a soul come along with them?"

"I won't even try to answer that," Patrick said. "To tell the truth, I've never given it an instant's thought until you just mentioned it."

Who had time to ponder such imponderables? Zero, obviously. And it seemed important to him.

"Think about it," Zero said. "Sims praying to a God who won't listen because they have no souls. Imagine believing in a God who doesn't believe in you. Tragic, don't you think?"

"Absolutely. But I wonder—"

The wail of a siren cut him off. He watched as an ambulance screamed into the parking lot across the street.

"You think that's for Romy?"

Zero's voice was close behind him. "I imagine so. I told her to give it her best performance."

They watched a pair of EMTs, a wiry male and a rather hefty woman, hurry inside. A few moments later they reemerged, pulled a stretcher from their rig, and hauled it inside.

"Wow," Patrick muttered. "She must be bucking for an Oscar."

He kept his tone light but felt a twinge of anxiety at the way those EMTs were hustling. A long ten minutes later they exited, wheeling the stretcher between them. But it wasn't empty this trip. Patrick could make out a slim figure in the blanket. Had to be Romy. He noticed that her head was swathed in gauze . . . with a crimson stain seeping through.

"Shit!" he cried, fear stabbing him as he reached for the door handle. "She's bleeding!"

"Wait!" he heard Zero say, but he was already out and moving toward the street.

No way he could sit in a van and watch Romy be wheeled into an ambulance by strangers when she was hurt and bleeding. Her gaze flicked his way as he dashed into the parking lot. When he saw her hand snake out from under the blanket and surreptitiously wave him off, he slowed his approach. And when she gave him a quick thumbs-up sign, he veered off and headed for the office building. He waited inside until the ambulance wailed off, then crossed back to the van.

"She seems okay," he said as he climbed back into the driver seat.

"Wonderful," replied the voice from the dim rear.

"But what the hell happened in there?" He threw the shift into forward and took off in pursuit of the ambulance. "She was supposed to stand clear and fake being hurt. How the hell did she cut her head open?"

"I should have foreseen this," Zero said. "This is so Romy."

"What do you mean?"

"Don't you understand? She had to make it real. She had to send a message to Manassas and SimGen and whoever else is involved that she's ready to bleed for her beliefs."

"Sheesh," Patrick muttered.

"Isn't she wonderful."

It wasn't a question. In that moment Patrick realized that the mysterious Zero, although "unavailable," was as smitten with Romy Cadman as he was.

"What is it about her?" Patrick said. "I mean, you're obviously taken by her, and I confess I'm drawn to her—"

"Drawn?"

"Like a moth to a searchlight. And then that guy Portero this morning—"

"Luca Portero? The SimGen security chief?"

"That's the one. He's got it bad for her. Might as well have written it on his forehead in DayGlo orange. What is it about Romy Cadman?"

"Simple: Her purity."

Patrick didn't have to ask. He knew Zero wasn't talking about virginity. He was talking about heart, about purpose.

"I hear you. But Portero didn't strike me as the kind who'd go for that."

"Some men approach purity like Romy's simply to protect it from harm; and some wish to draw closer in the hope that it will rub off on them or somehow cleanse them; and others want to possess it merely to defile it and extinguish it because it reminds them of what they have become, as opposed to what they could have been."

Patrick glanced Zero's way in the rearview. He'd obviously given a lot of thought to it. Deep thought.

"Well, I guess we know where Portero fits in that scheme."

"I think we do."

"But how about you?"

A long pause, then Zero said, "If my circumstances were different, I'd be content merely to warm myself in her glow. And if I couldn't do that I'd settle for curling up outside her door every night to keep her safe from trespassers."

Patrick swallowed, unexpectedly moved.

"You know, Zero," he said, his voice a tad hoarse, "I've got to admit I've had my doubts about you. Major, heavy-duty doubts. But now . . ."

"Now?"

Patrick didn't know quite what to say. Any man who could pinpoint Romy as Zero had, and who could not only feel about her the way he'd described, but come out and say it . . .

"You're all right."

Lame, but the best he could do at the moment. At least it was sincere. Romy would have appreciated that.

8

Patrick parted the curtains that separated Romy's treatment area from the rest of the emergency room. She sat on the edge of a gurney, her head swathed in fresh gauze—but no seepage this time. She looked pale and tired, but even so, to Patrick she was a vision.

"How are you feeling?"

A wan smile. "I've got a killer headache but I'll survive."

He leaned close. "How'd you get hurt?"

"You've heard the expression, 'Shit happens'? Well—"

Patrick clapped his hands over his ears. "The 'S' word! Saints preserve us!" He wanted to throw his arms around her but made do with seating himself next to her on the gurney. "Seriously. What happened?"

"This lighting fixture fell from the ceiling and clocked me on the noggin; things get a little fuzzy after that. Doctor said he put seventeen stitches into my scalp and that I should—"

"Seventeen!" The number horrified him.

"It's not as bad as it sounds. He said he placed them close together to keep the scar thin."

Scar? "Jesus, Romy—"

She smiled. "It's not like I'm going to look like the bride of Frankenstein. It cut my scalp, way up above the hairline. Once the hair grows back where they shaved it, no one will know, not even me."

Relief seeped through Patrick. The lighting fixture had been his idea. If it had left Romy disfigured . . .

"Why, Romy?"

"Relax, will you. I got a tetanus shot out of it, and a free ride in a red-light-running ambulance. It's no biggee, Patrick. Really."

"Is to me. Zero too." Patrick had driven him back to the garage, then rushed here. "He wants me to call him as soon as—"

"I'll call him."

"How many days are they going to keep you?"

"Days? More like minutes. They're finishing up my paperwork now."

"You're kidding!" Patrick realized his knowledge of medicine was just this side of nothing, but wasn't it standard procedure to admit a head-trauma patient for observation, at least overnight? "They're letting you go?"

"Be real, will you. It's just a cut on my head. I can—"

"Excuse me," said a male voice.

Patrick looked up and saw a dark-haired man in a gray suit standing between the parted curtains.

"Are you her doctor?" Patrick said. If so he was going to warn him about the malpractice risks of releasing Romy too early.

The man flashed a collector's edition set of pearlies. "Not a chance. I'm an attorney and I'm looking for the woman who was injured in the Manassas Ventures offices this morning."

Patrick stared at him. He'd met his share of ambulance chasers, but this guy really lived up to the name.

"That would be me." Romy shook her head. "But I don't need a lawyer. I've—"

"You're absolutely right. And that's precisely why I'm here." He handed Romy a card. "Harold Rudner. I represent Manassas Ventures." He set his briefcase on the gurney and popped its latches. "The company called me the instant it heard of this unfortunate incident and instructed me to find you and compensate you immediately for the pain and inconvenience you have suffered."

"Compensate me?"

He lifted the briefcase lid, removed a slip of paper, and extended it toward Romy.

"Exactly. Although your injury resulted from shoddy work by remodeling contractors, Manassas is taking full responsibility and offering you this to ease your distress."

Romy took the slip and stared at it. "A check? For a hundred thousand dollars."

"Yes." He pulled a sheaf of papers from the briefcase. "And all you need do to have your name written on the pay-to-the-order-of line is sign this release absolving Manassas Ventures of all liability and refrain from any future—"

"Wow!" Patrick said, genuinely impressed. "Hit her while she's still dazed from the terrible concussive impact of her life-threatening head injury, then shove a check under her nose and tell her all those zeroes can be hers if she'll just sign away her legal rights to just compensation for an injury that might affect her quality of life for years, maybe decades, perhaps permanently. You *are* a smoothy."

Romy and Rudner were staring at him.

Finally Rudner spoke. "Are you her lawyer?"

"I am a very close personal friend who just happens to be an attorney."

Rudner turned to Romy. "I am offering you far more than you could hope to receive from any jury."

"We'll see about that," Patrick said. "One hundred thousand dollars barely scratches the surface of the amount this unfortunate woman deserves for her pain and suffering."

Romy smiled and handed back the check. Rudner took it with a sad shake of his head.

"You're making a big mistake," he told her. "One you'll regret when a jury offers you only a fraction of this—one third of which will go to your attorney. This could be all yours, every cent of it."

Romy's hands flew to her mouth as she gave Patrick a wide-eyed stare. "Oh, Patrick! Am I making a terrible mistake? You know how I depend on your wisdom. Tell me. I don't know what to do!"

Patrick had to look away. It took all his will to keep a straight face. When he had control, he turned back to her and lowered his voice an octave. "Trust me, my dear. I am well versed in these matters. You deserve much, much more."

"All . . . all right," she said, her voice faltering. "If you say so."

Rudner shook his head again and closed his briefcase. As he lifted it off the gurney he turned to Patrick.

"And you have the nerve to call *me* a smoothy."

As soon as he was gone they both doubled over in silent laughter.

"'Terrible concussive impact'?" Romy gasped, red faced.

Patrick countered with, "'You know how I depend on your wisdom'? I thought I was going to get a hernia!"

She pressed her hands against her temples. "Oh, I shouldn't laugh! It makes my headache worse!"

Patrick looked at her. "I know this is serious business, but I couldn't resist. That was fun."

She frowned. "Do you think he knew who we were?"

"Not a clue. He's a hired gun." Patrick shook his head, still amazed at how quickly the company had responded. "A hundred grand for a cut head offered to someone they might just as easily have charged with trespassing. If this is any indication of how badly Manassas Ventures wants to avoid the legal system, I think we're onto something."

9

Sussex County, NJ

"So," Mercer Sinclair said, "the missing globulin farmers have surfaced." He'd chosen that word deliberately but his little pun went unappreciated by his audience. So he added, "Literally."

That at least elicited a smile from Able Voss.

Mercer had invited the usual crew—Voss, Portero, and Ellis—to his office to discuss the matter. He had his agenda for the meeting posted in a corner of the computer monitor embedded in the ebony expanse of his desk while his custom news service scrolled headlines tailored to his topics of interest.

"Post mortem ain't back yet," Voss said, "but the M-E's on notice to copy us immediately with any and all results."

"I'm told the bodies looked like they'd been in the river about a week."

Voss nodded. "All three of them shackled together and weighted down. But the Hudson's gotta way of returning some of the gifts it gets. Looks like these SLA boys took 'em for a ride that night, shot them in the head, then dumped them before sunup."

"But not before torturing them," Ellis said.

Mercer glanced at his brother. Ellis hadn't missed a meeting in months now. Maybe his latest anti-depressant cocktail was working. Mercer knew he should be glad about that but he wasn't. The closer Ellis was to catatonia, the easier he was to deal with.

"Yep, I heard that too," Voss said. "Cigarette burns, fingernails tore off." He grimaced. "Ugly stuff."

"They were globulin farmers, Able," Mercer said, unable to keep the scorn from his tone. "Somebody improved the gene pool by removing them."

"Don't get me wrong, son. I ain't no fan of their sort. Riddin the world of their kind is all fine and good. But torture? Ain't no call to torture no one, son. No one. I think we're dealin with some real sick puppies here."

"Which segues very neatly into the reason for our meeting: the 'sick puppies' who call themselves the Sim Liberation Army. It's been a week since they raided that globulin farm and no one knows any more about them today than they did then. And where are the sims they supposedly wanted to free?"

He turned to his chief of security who had yet to say a word. Mercer hadn't picked Portero. He'd been *assigned* to SimGen as security chief. But he'd looked into the man's background. A self-made man, starting off as a street urchin with an Italian first name in a mostly Mexican border-town in Arizona, father unknown, mother of very dubious reputation—oh, hell why not say it? She was the town whore. As soon as he was old enough he joined the Army and apparently found his métier.

"Mr. Portero, if the NYPD is at a loss, surely your people have the resources to pick up the slack, don't you think?"

Portero shrugged. "We're looking into it."

"This needs more than mere looking into, Mr. Portero. We need to track them down. It's vitally important that SimGen be recognized as the true guardians and protectors of sims, not some group of murderous radicals."

Portero said, "The longer they go undetected, the lower the odds of finding them. And so far they seem to have pulled off a perfect disappearing act."

"Which means what?"

"That they're probably professionals—well-funded professionals. Which makes me wonder if they might not be connected to that lawyer Patrick Sullivan."

"Why on earth would you think that?" Ellis said.

"It's not a stretch. A quarter of a million dollars appeared out of the blue to keep his unionization case going just when it was ready to fall apart. And I saw him and the Cadman woman outside the globulin farm the morning after this SLA demolished it."

Cadman? Mercer thought. Didn't I just see that name? He reversed the scroll on his newsclips as Ellis spoke up.

"On the contrary, Portero. It's *quite* a stretch. People who try to use the legal system to seek a solution don't suddenly leap to murder and arson."

Portero's face remained impassive as he replied. "Perhaps Sullivan became a bit testy after his clients were put down."

Ellis stared at him. "You lousy piece of—"

"Gentlemen, gentlemen," Voss said, shifting his considerable bulk in his seat and raising his hands. "We're not the enemy here. The enemy is out there."

"Really?" Ellis said. "Sometimes I wonder."

Cadman . . . Mercer kept searching his screen. There. Found it. A suit against Manassas. He smiled. He'd long ago embraced his anal-completist nature because it so often paid unexpected dividends. Like now: he'd entered 'Manassas Ventures' as a search string long ago when he'd begun using the service and this was the first hit he'd ever seen. He clicked on the abstract to bring up the full article; he frowned as he skimmed it. This wasn't good. Pretty damn disturbing in fact. But it would give Portero a swift boot in the ass. And anything that bothered Portero wasn't entirely bad.

"This is interesting," Mercer said. "Someone is suing Manassas Ventures."

He noticed a stiffening of Portero's parade-rest stance. "What for?"

"Let's see . . . no dollar amount given, just 'unspecified compensatory and punitive damages.' "

"No, I mean the reason for the suit."

"Lots of things. Here's just a sample: 'physical injury, pain, suffering, mental anguish and trauma, unpleasant mental reactions including fright, horror, worry, disgrace, embarrassment, indignity, ridicule, grief, shame, humiliation, anger, and outrage.' "

Portero snorted. "Probably a stubbed toe. They'll put a check in front of him and he'll go away."

"I doubt it. It's not a him. It's a her named Cadman. Romilda Cadman."

Portero's smug reptile mask dropped, just for a second, and the flash of uncertainty Mercer caught behind it was worth a million shares of SimGen.

"The OPRR inspector lady?" Voss said. "The one who funded Sullivan's sim case? What the *hell*?"

"Care to guess what attorney is representing her?"

"I don't have to," Voss said. "Gotta be Sullivan."

Mercer noted that Portero's dumbfounded look had surrendered to tight-lipped anger. He glanced at his brother, expecting some sort of comment, but Ellis remained silent, his expression unreadable.

"Right," Mercer said. "Patrick Sullivan again."

"This makes no sense." Portero's voice was even softer than usual. "What can they possibly hope to gain from this? Are they that desperate for cash?"

"Oh, I doubt money's got a thing to do with this," Voss said. "It will take them years to get a decision, and even if they win, more years before they ever see a dime. No, instead of thinking about money, we should be asking why the man who harassed SimGen about unionizing sims is now harassing the venture capital company that helped put SimGen in business."

The question disturbed Mercer as well. The gnawing sense of malignant forces converging on him had receded after the withdrawal of the sim unionization suit, but now it returned, nibbling at him again.

"You're the lawyer," he said to Voss. "You tell us."

"I think he wants to use the discovery procedures of a civil action to dissect Manassas Ventures' workings—its board of directors, its assets and liabilities, the whole tamale."

"But why Manassas? Beyond owning a bundle of SimGen stock, it has no direct link to us."

"Not anymore, but it used to. Obviously he's sniffed out something and he's going after it."

"Maybe it's just a fishing expedition."

"Could be, but why in that particular pond? And let's face it, Manassas is such a well-stocked pond, he just might hook something."

No one spoke then. The idea that anyone would want to lift the Manassas Ventures rock and inspect what was crawling around beneath it had never occurred to Mercer.

He sighed and looked at Portero. "Well, Manassas Ventures is in your people's bailiwick. I'm sure they can handle this."

"Wait a minute, wait a minute," Voss said, holding up a hand before Portero could reply. "Before we start talking about stuff I don't want to hear, why don't you just buy her off?"

Portero stared at him. "Buy her off? You don't know this woman. I spent days with her during the OPRR inspection and let me tell you, she is not for sale."

Voss grinned. "Sure she is, son. I've waded through truckloads of bullshit in my day, but I've learned one thing always holds true: Everybody's got a price tag. Some hide it better'n others, but you look hard enough, you'll find it. Your folks've got pockets deep as a well to China. You have them tell her to name a price, and then you meet it. And that'll be it. You'll see."

But Portero was shaking his head. "I don't think there's enough money in the world."

Mercer was surprised by something in his tone. It sounded like admiration.

10

Manhattan

Zero had asked Romy and Patrick to come over to the West Side garage. Romy was already there when Patrick arrived. With her oversized sunglasses hiding her shiners, and her baseball cap covering her stitched-up scalp, she looked none the worse for wear.

Patrick asked her how she was doing, and of course she told him fine. She was always "fine."

"Quite an interesting picture you took," Zero said, handing Romy an eight-by-ten color print.

It was hard to see the photo in the dimly lit garage, so Patrick craned his head over Romy's shoulder for a better look, but found himself gazing at the nape of her neck instead, focusing on the gentle wisps of fine dark hair trailing along the curve. He leaned closer, drinking her scent, barely resisting the urge to press his lips against the soft white skin . . .

"That's him, all right," Romy said. "He ducked away so fast I wasn't sure I caught him. Does he have a name?"

"Yes. It took me a while to trace him but—"

"Christ!" Patrick said, pointing to a spot at the rear end of the ceiling. "Who's that?"

He'd glanced up and caught a flicker of movement above and beyond Zero, at the point where a ladder embedded in the rear wall of the garage ran up to a square opening in the ceiling. He could swear he'd seen a pair of eyes peering out at them from within that darkness.

Zero didn't turn to look. "Where?"

"There! In that opening! I saw someone!"

The opening was empty now, but he knew what he'd seen.

"I'm sure you did," Zero told him. "But it was no one you need concern yourself with at the moment. Now—"

"Wait a minute, wait a minute," Patrick said, walking over to the ladder. "If someone's up there listening, I want to know who it is."

"Someone's up there *guarding*," Romy said. "Please, Patrick. Let it go for now."

He didn't like letting it go, but short of climbing up there and entering that patch of night—something he had no inclination to do—Patrick didn't see that he had much choice.

"All right," he said, turning back. "You were saying?"

Zero said, "The man in the photo looked Japanese to me so I scanned him into a computer and had it comb the databases of the Japanese government and major Japanese corporations." He held up a printout of a full-face photo of someone who bore a passing resemblance to the man in Romy's shot. "This came back with a sixty-three percent confidence match."

"That's him," Romy said without hesitation.

"You're sure? The computer wasn't."

"Don't care. I saw him live and that's him."

"Fine," Patrick said. "Now . . . who's him?"

"Yoshi Hirai, Ph.D.," Zero said. "Top recombinant man for Arata-jinruien Corporation."

"Which is . . .?" Patrick had never heard of the company.

"A division of Kaze Group and one of SimGen's potential competitors. They want to raise their own sims but so far haven't met with any success. They even started a dummy corporation to pirate SimGen's sim genome but were caught. They'll do anything to cut into the sim market."

"What was a creep like that doing at the fire?" Romy asked.

"Exactly what I'd like to know. Is the SLA Japanese? But why hijack sims when they can lease as many as they want? And why these globulin farm sims?"

"Never mind why," Romy said. "How about where? Where are those sims? That's my concern. I hope they don't end up like their farmers, or get spirited off to Japan. We'll never find them."

11

Riverside Park

Meerm so very sad. Live all alone in bush. Walk night, hide day. Find clothes, dirty, smelly, but warm. Wear three shirt and two pant. Steal blanket. Carry all night while search food.

Pain wake Meerm in bush home. Dark come now. Many people walk. Meerm know must stay hid till late. Meerm so hungry. Peek out bush. Ver near big round building made stone. See lady point, say, "Granztoom."

Meerm not know what granztoom.

Meerm move along wall, stay dark spot. Climb to street. Put blanket over head and walk. Keep face down, look sidewalk. So fraid people hurt if see Meerm, but people walk fast, not look Meerm.

Meerm look light-front place people eat. Can find food in dark behind. But see no place yet. Street dark. Hear noise behind. Meerm so scare, push against wall, turn. Building door open. Sim come out. Two sim, three sim, many sim. Meerm watch as more sim than count line up straight at curb.

Meerm see bus come and all sim go in. Meerm so cold, so hurt, so lone. Meerm drop blanket and go behind last sim. Climb step, sit empty seat. Bus dark and warm. Meerm curl up, close eye.

12

Westchester County, NY

Patrick's breath steamed in the night air as he strolled across the rear lawn of Beacon Ridge toward the sim barrack. He'd been back only once since the night of the poisoning. He wasn't sure exactly why he'd come here tonight. He was in the area to sign some papers dealing with his property—someone had made an offer on what was left of his home and he'd accepted—and thought of Tome. He decided to stop by and see how the old sim was doing.

As he reached for the knob on the barrack door it opened and out stepped Holmes Carter. He jerked his portly frame to a halt, obviously startled.

"Sullivan?"

"Carter. Fancy meeting you here."

Carter didn't offer to shake hands, neither did Patrick. They'd reached a détente but that didn't make them friends.

"I was just about to say that myself," Carter replied. "You're trespassing, you know."

"Yeah, I know. But ease up. I'm not looking for new clients. Just visiting an old one. Promise."

"Tome?"

"Yeah." Patrick noticed Carter staring at him from under his protruding forehead, saying nothing. "Something wrong?"

"I guess you could say I'm amazed. I figured since the sims dropped the union idea and were of no further use to you, we'd never see you again."

"That's usually the way it goes with client-attorney relationships, but these were special clients."

Another long stare from Carter. He was making Patrick uncomfortable.

"You're full of surprises, aren't you, Sullivan." Then he sighed. "Maybe it's a good thing you're here. Tome isn't doing too well."

Aw, no. "Is he sick?"

"I had a vet check him and she says no. He does his washroom duties, but just barely. He's listless, eating just enough to stay alive, and spending all of his free time in his bunk."

It occurred to Patrick that Holmes Carter seemed to know an awful lot about this aging sim.

"What brings you down to the barracks? Never knew you to be one to mix with the help."

He looked away. "Just checking up on him. So sue me, I'm worried."

Now it was Patrick's turn to stare. He remembered how Carter had pitched in to help the poisoned sims, and now this.

"You're no slouch in the surprise department yourself, Holmes." This just might be the first time he'd ever addressed the man by his first name.

"The board wants him declared D and replaced. I was giving him a pep talk but I'm not getting through. Want to take a crack at him?"

Patrick knew that if Tome were human he'd have been offered grief counseling after the killings. The poor old guy must be really hurting.

He stepped past Carter into the barrack.

"I'll give it a shot."

With Holmes Carter following, Patrick wandered through the familiar front room, past the long dining tables and battered old easy chairs clustered around the TVs in two of the corners. The gathered sims glanced at him, then returned to what they were doing. He thought of the joyous welcomes he used to see every time he stuck his head in the door, but most of those sims were dead or still at work, finishing up in the club kitchen.

But wait . . . he remembered one sim, a caddie . . .

"Where's Deek?" he said.

Carter glanced around. "I don't see him. Might be sitting outside. The other survivors seemed to have bounced back, but not Tome."

That's because he was the patriarch, Patrick thought.

He proceeded into the rear area and looked around. The sleeping area was dimly lit; his gaze wandered up and down the rows of bunk beds, searching for one that was occupied.

"Left rear corner," Carter said. "Lower bunk."

Patrick started forward, puzzled. He'd already looked at that bunk and had thought it was empty. But now he could see a shape under the covers, barely raising them, curled and facing the wall.

"Tome?" he said.

The shape turned and Patrick recognized Tome's face as it broke into a wide smile.

"Mist Sulliman?" The old sim slipped from under the covers and rose to his feet beside his bed. "So good to see."

Patrick's throat constricted at the sight of Tome's stooped, emaciated form. Wasn't he eating at all?

"Good to see you too, Tome."

He held out his hand and, after a second's hesitation, Tome reached his own forward.

"You come see Mist Carter?" Tome said as they shook hands.

"No, Tome. I came by to see you." Patrick saw something in Tome's eyes when he said that, something beyond gratitude. "But Mister Carter tells me you're not doing well. He says you spend all your free time in bed. Are you sick, Tome? Is there anything I can do?"

"Not sick, no," he said, shaking his head. "Tome sad. See dead sim ever time walk through eat room. Can't stay. Tired all time."

Patrick nodded, understanding. Tome had to go on living in the building where the sims he'd considered his family were murdered, had to eat in the room where they died. No wonder he was wasting away.

Then Patrick had an idea, one he knew would cause complications in his life. But the sense of having failed Tome and his makeshift family had been dogging Patrick since that terrible and ugly night, and helping him now wasn't something he merely wanted to do, it was something he needed to do.

"You know what you need?" Patrick said. "You need a change of scenery. Wait here."

He went back to Carter, pulled him into a corner and, after a ten-minute negotiation, the deal was set.

"All right, Tome," he said, returning to the bunk. "Pack up your stuff. You're going on a vacation."

Tome's brow furrowed. "Vay-kaysh . . ."

Poor old guy didn't even know what the word meant. Patrick decided not to try to explain because this wasn't going to be a real vacation anyway. Simply removing Tome from the barracks might be enough, but Patrick thought the old sim would want to feel useful.

"You're going to stay with me for a while. I've got a brand new office and I need a helper."

Tome straightened, his eyes brighter already. "Tome work for Mist Sulliman? But club own—"

"That's all taken care of."

Patrick had convinced Carter to allow him to take over Tome's lease payments for a month or so. As club president, Carter had the authority, and the board couldn't squawk too much because it wasn't costing the club a penny. The lease payments wouldn't be cheap but Patrick had all that money left in the Sim Defense Fund and figured it wouldn't be a misappropriation to use some of it to help a sim.

As for keeping Tome busy, the old sim had taught himself to read so it shouldn't be a big stretch for him to learn to file.

"Unless of course," Patrick said, "you'd rather stay here."

"No, no," Tome said, waddling over to a locker. "Tome come."

As Patrick watched him stuff his worldly belongings in a black plastic trash bag, he wondered at his own impulsiveness. He'd been planning to convert the second of the two bedrooms in his newfound apartment into a study, but he guessed that could wait. Let Tome have it for a month or so. Who knew how much of his abbreviated lifespan the old sim had left?

Not as if it's going to interfere with my sex life, Patrick thought, thinking of the persistently elusive Romy.

"Tome ready, Mist Sulliman," the sim said, standing before him with straightened spine and thin shoulders thrown back.

"Let's go then," Patrick said, smiling at himself as much as at Tome. He felt like Cary Grant teaching Gunga Din to drill. Not a bad feeling; not bad at all. "Time to see the world, Mr. Tome."

13

Newark, NJ

"Hey, you sim."

Finger poke Meerm. Open eyes and see sim look in face.

"You new sim? You no work. Why you ride?"

"Cold. Hurt. Sick."

"Beece tell drive man."

"No!" Meerm sit up. Look out window. Bus on bridge cross water. Whisper, "No tell mans! Mans hurt Meerm!"

"Mans not hurt."

"Yes-yes! Mans hurt Meerm. Make Meerm sick. Please-please-please no tell mans!"

Other sim look round, say, "Okay. No tell mans." Sit next Meerm. "I Beece."

"I Meerm." Look window. "Where go?"

"Call Newark. Sim home there."

Ride and ride, then bus stop by big building. Meerm follow Beece and other sim out. Up stair to room of many bed, like room of many bed in burned home.

Meerm say, "Mans hurt here?"

"Mans no hurt. Mans feed. Sim sleep. Sim work morning."

Beece show Meerm empty bed. All other sim go eat. Meerm hide. Beece and other sim bring food. Meerm eat. Not yum-yum sick room food like old burned home but not garbage food.

Meerm sleep on empty bed. Warm. Fed. If only sick pain stop, Meerm be happy sim.

14

Manhattan

"Perrier?" Judy said. "Are my ears playing tricks or did I just hear you order a club soda?"

Ellis considered his ex wife. Judy was looking better than ever. With her perfectly coifed blond hair, her diamond bracelets, and her high-collared, long-sleeved, clinging pink dress made out of some sort of jersey material—Versace, he guessed, because she'd always loved Versace—she fit perfectly here at Tavern-On-The-Green. Judy was only two years his junior, but Ellis thought he must look like her father. She was enjoying her wealth from the divorce settlement. Far more than Ellis was enjoying his own billions.

"Yes," Ellis told her. "I've decided to take a vacation from alcohol."

"That's wonderful, Ellis." And he knew she meant it. The divorce had been amicable: Ellis had told her she could have anything she wanted. That said, she'd taken a lot less then she could have—more than the GNP of a number of small nations, to be sure, but still, she could have grabbed for so much more. "How long has this been going on?"

"Since the summer."

"What made you . . ."

"Lots of developments, lots of things happening. Things I want to keep an eye on."

"And Mercer? How's he?"

"The same. Eats, sleeps, and drinks the business. Still obsessed with SimGen's profits and its image. Someday he'll look around and wonder where his life has gone." He leaned closer and lowered his voice. "Did you hold on to all that SimGen stock from the settlement?"

Her brows knitted. "Yes. Why?"

"Wait till after the next earnings report, take advantage of the bounce, then dump it."

"Is something wrong?"

"Things might become . . . unsettled. I want you and the kids protected. But mum's the word. Just sell quietly and stick it all in T-notes, okay?"

She set her lips and nodded.

"Good." He straightened, put on a happy face, and looked around the table. "But enough about me and Mercer and business. This is a celebration." He turned to Robbie. "How's the birthday going so far?"

His son shrugged, mixing a typical fifteen-year-old's studied nonchalance with embarrassment at being out on the town with his folks and his younger sister on his birthday. He was underdressed in denims for the occasion, but that was to be expected of a boy his age; his buzz-cut hair revealed a bumpy skull. Hardly attractive,

Ellis thought, but it was the style. So was the turquoise stud in Robbie's left earlobe. At least he showed no signs of a splice, and Ellis prayed he never would. He realized it was a teenager's duty to irk his parents, but he just wished Robbie would find his own ways rather than galloping after the herd.

"Okay, I guess."

Ellis smiled. He wasn't making any appreciable progress developing the new sim line he so desperately wanted, but he was feeling good about himself nonetheless, better than he had in years, and he wanted to share it. Only on rare state occasions did they get together as a family, but he'd used Robbie's fifteenth birthday as a reason, and it was as good an excuse as any.

"Just okay?" Ellis said. "This is your favorite restaurant, right?"

He gestured around at the sunny, glass-walled Terrace Room with its hand-carved plaster ceiling and panoramic view of Central Park. The park was more impressive when in bloom, but even here in late fall he found a certain stark, Wyethesque beauty in the denuded trees. The Terrace Room's seating capacity was 150. Today it seated only four. Ellis had rented out the entire space for the family luncheon. And for afterwards he had four precious front-row tickets to *Wordplay!*, the hot new musical comedy everyone said was a must-see. Then dinner at Le Cirque, followed by a Knicks game in the SimGen skybox.

"I can't wait to see the play!" Julie said.

She was thirteen and the light of Ellis's life. Judy had dressed her in a plaid wool skirt and a white blouse. Julie's pod backpack was suede, sporting the Dooney &

Bourke logo. Robbie was an intelligent kid, but Julie was brilliant. She had a wonderful future ahead of her.

"You just want to see Joey Dozier," Robbie sneered.

"Who's he?" Ellis said, fully aware he was a teen heartthrob who'd moved from a hit TV sitcom to lead in a Broadway play. "Never heard of him."

Julie got a dreamy look in her eyes. "He's *gorgeous!*" she said, as if that explained it all.

Ellis started to laugh but it died in his throat as he saw the small crowd of sign-carrying protesters appear at the Terrace Room windows. Their chant of "Free the sims! Free the sims!" began to echo through the glass.

The tuxedoed maitre d' hurried to Ellis's side.

"I'm so sorry, Mr. Sinclair. I've called the police. They will be here in a few minutes."

Ellis looked around the table. Judy was ignoring them, Julie was watching, fascinated, and Robbie, the birthday boy, looked ready to crawl under the table. A glance back toward the main area of the restaurant showed some of the staff, humans and sims, standing on the threshold, watching.

"How did they know I'd be here?" Ellis asked, furious. He'd booked the whole room just to avoid an incident, even used a pseudonym.

"Someone must have recognized you."

Pretty fast work, considering he left all the public appearances to Mercer. Probably someone on the Tavern staff. However it had happened, he wasn't going to let them ruin the day he had planned.

He pushed back his chair and rose. "I'll handle this."

"Ellis, no!" Judy said, placing a hand on his arm.

"Mr. Sinclair, the police—"

"Could take a while to get here. In the meantime I want to talk to these people."

He crossed to a door leading out to the lawn and stepped through. The shouting grew louder as the crowd—a three-to-one ratio of women to men—recognized him. He stood impassively for a moment or two, then raised his hands.

When they quieted enough for him to be heard he said, "Please. I'm trying to have lunch with my family."

Cries of "Aaaaaw!" and "Pity the poor man!" rose, and one woman stepped forward to snarl, "Yeah! Eating lunch served by slave labor!"

Ellis decided not to waste his breath instructing her about the difference between wait staff and bus staff. He'd noticed something interesting about a number of the protesters.

"If this is supposed to accomplish something," he told them, "I assure you it won't. Perhaps a more sincere group might make a point, but not a bunch of hypocrites."

Ellis stepped forward into the gasps of "What!" and "You bastard!" and "What right?" and pointed to the snarling woman's handbag.

"Virducci, right?"

Her only reply was a stunned look.

"Sim made!" Ellis pivoted and jabbed a finger at the insignia on a man's windbreaker. "Tammy Montain—sim made!" As he slipped deeper into the throng, pointing out all the popular labels that used sim labor, crying "Sim made!" over and over, he knew he should be careful. But these people angered him, and not simply because they'd interrupted his lunch.

Finally he was back where he'd started and could see by their expressions and averted eyes that he'd taken the steam out of them.

"How can you be part of the solution when you're part of the problem?" he said, knowing it was a cliché but knowing too that it would hit home. "You really want to 'free the sims'? The fastest way is to boycott any company that uses them as labor. Companies understand one thing: the bottom line. If that's falling off because they use sim labor, then they're going to *stop* using sim labor. It's as simple as that. But you can't show up here wearing sim-made clothes and shoes and accessories and expect anyone with a brain to take you seriously. If you're sincere about this you're going to have to make some sacrifices, you're going to have to let the Joneses have the more prestigious sim-made car, the more fashionable sim-made sweater. Otherwise, you're just blowing smoke."

Ellis stepped back inside and closed the door behind him. He had no idea what the protesters would do next, but the question was made moot by the arrival of half a dozen cops who began herding them off.

He returned to the table to find his family staring at him.

"Dad," Robbie said, wide eyed. "You were great!"

"Ellis?" Judy said. Ellis noticed a tremor in her voice, and were those . . .? Yes, she had tears in her eyes. "For a moment there you were like . . . like you used to be."

He looked into her moist blue eyes. God, he wanted her back, more than anything in the world.

"I don't know if I can ever be like I used to be, Judy," he said, knowing his soul was scarred beyond repair, "but if things go right, if a few things happen the way I hope they will, I should be able to present a reasonable facsimile."

"But Dad," Robbie was saying, "you were, like, telling them how to, like, to screw your own company."

Ellis put on a pensive expression. "You know, Robbie, now that you mention it, I believe I was. I'll have to be more careful in the future."

He noticed Julie staring at the sim busboy as he removed her empty shrimp cocktail cup. Her gaze stayed fixed on him until he'd exited the room, then she turned to her father.

"Will sims ever evolve into humans?" she said, looking up at him with her mother's huge blue eyes.

Ellis stared at her, momentarily dumb.

"She's studying evolution in school," Judy offered.

Ellis cleared his throat and controlled the sudden urge to run from the room. He'd rather be off the subject of sims—this was Robbie's birthday after all—and especially off their evolutionary genetics, but how could he not answer the jewel of his life?

"Do *you* think they will?"

"Well," she said slowly, "we humans evolved from chimps, and sims are a mix of chimps and humans, so won't sims evolve into humans someday?"

"No," Ellis said, choosing his words carefully. "You see, humans didn't evolve from chimps; chimps and humans are primates and both evolved from a common primate ancestor, an ape that had evolved from the monkeys."

"A gorilla?"

"No. Gorillas branched off earlier. Let's just call our common ancestor the mystery primate."

Julie grinned. "Why call him '*mystery* primate'?"

"Because we haven't found his bones yet. But we don't need to. Genetics tells the story. So even though we may never identify the mystery primate's remains, we know he existed and we know that at some point millions of years ago, whether because of a flood or a continental upheaval or climactic changes in Africa, a segment of the mystery primate population became separated from the larger main body. This smaller group of primates wound up stranded in a hotter, drier environment, probably in northeast Africa; some theories say it was an island, but whatever the specifics, the important point is they were cut off from all the other jungle-dwelling primates. And there, under pressure to adapt to their new environment, they began to evolve in their own direction."

"But didn't the mystery primates in the jungle evolve too?"

"Of course, but because they were in an environment they were used to, there was no need for much change, so they evolved more slowly, and in a different direction: toward what we now call chimpanzees. Meanwhile the primates in the separated group, in a drier, savanna-like environment, were changing: they were growing taller, their skin was losing its hair and learning to sweat in the hotter temperatures; and because they were no longer in a lush jungle where food was hanging from every other tree, they had to learn to hunt to keep from starving. This added extra protein to their diet which meant they could afford to enlarge a very important organ that needs lots of protein to grow. Do you know what that organ is?"

"The brain," Julie said.

"You are *smart*," he told her. "Absolutely right. The sum of all these changes meant that they were evolving into hominids."

"Humans, right?"

"Humans are hominids, true, but it took millions of years for the first hominids to evolve into *Homo sapiens*."

"But once they got back to the jungle, couldn't they get back together with the mystery primates?"

Bright as Julie was, Ellis wondered how far he could delve into the intricacies of evolutionary drift with a thirteen-year-old. He paused, looking for an analogy. He knew she played the cello in her school orchestra . . . maybe she could understand if he related evolution to music.

"Think of DNA as a magnificent symphony, amazingly complex even though it is composed with only four notes. Every gene is a movement, and every base pair is a musical note within that movement. So if one of those base pairs is out of sequence, the melody can go wrong, become discordant. If enough are out of place, it can ruin the entire symphony. But sometimes changes can work to the benefit of the symphony.

"Imagine the sheet music for a symphony arriving in a city far from where it was composed. The local musicians look at it and say, 'No one around here is going to like this section, nor that movement; we'd better change them.' And they do. And then that version is shipped off to another city even farther away, and those local musicians find they must make further changes to satisfy their audience. And on it goes, until the symphony is radically different from what was on the original sheets.

"This is what happened to the hominid's DNA symphony. It was changed by a different environment; but the chimp DNA symphony never left its hometown, so it changed relatively little. And because they'd been separated, with the genes of one group never having a chance to mix with the genes of the other, each group kept evolving in its own direction, causing their genomes to drift further and further apart.

"At some point millions of years ago both groups reached the stage where neither was a mystery primate anymore. By the time the hominids started spreading into different areas of Africa, it was too late for a reunion. The hominids were playing heavy metal blues, while the chimps still sounded like Bach. They couldn't play together. Too many changes. One of the most obvious was the fusion of two primate chromosomes in the hominids, leaving them with twenty-three pairs instead of the twenty-four their jungle cousins still carried."

"But sims have only twenty-two pairs, right?" Julie said. "What happened—?"

"That's way too long a story for now," Ellis said quickly. "Suffice it to say that the two groups had evolved so far apart that they could no longer have children together. Once that happened, their evolutionary courses were separated forever. So you see, a chimpanzee cannot evolve into a human any more than a human . . ."

His voice dried up.

Julie said, "But that doesn't mean a sim won't evolve into a human."

"Sims are different, Julie. They *can't* evolve. Ever. To evolve you must be able to have children, and sims can't. Each sim is cloned from a stock of identical cell cultures. They are all genetically equal. Evolution involves genetic changes occurring over many generations, but sims have no generations, therefore no evolution."

"This is pretty heavy luncheon chatter, don't you think?" Judy said.

Ellis was grateful for the interruption.

"Your mother's right." He chucked Julie gently under the chin. "We can continue this another time. But did I answer your question?"

"Sure," Julie said with a smile. "Sims will always be stuck being sims."

Ellis stared past his daughter at the sim returning his bus tray to the nearby fold-up stand.

Not if I can help it, he thought.

15

Newark

Meerm here some days now. Little happy here.

Still tired-sick and hurt-belly-sick, sometime cold-sick and hot-sick. No more cold-hungry. Have place live, have food. Lonely in day when all sim go work. Meerm try help by clean and make bed. Must be quiet. Not let man downstair, man call Benny, know Meerm here.

Shhh! Benny come now. Benny come upstair ever day.

Meerm rush closet. Hide. Peek through door crack. See Benny walk round and open window. Come once ever morning. Always talk self.

"Damn monkeys!" Benny say. "Bad enough I gotta play nursemaid to 'em all night, but why they have to stink so bad."

Benny open all window, then close all. Ver cold while window open, even in closet. Meerm shiver.

Benny leave and warm start come again. Meerm stay closet and wait. Better when sim come. Sim laugh, talk, bring Meerm food, not tell Benny. Meerm lonely till then. Wait Beece.

Beece friend. Try make better when Meerm hurt. Beece say Meerm need doctor. No doctor! Not for Meerm! Doctor hurt Meerm. No doctor! Beece say okay but not like. Meerm can tell.

Meerm little happy here. Meerm stay.

16

Manhattan

Patrick paced his new office space, waiting for Romy. He'd asked her to show up early for their meeting with the Manassas Ventures attorneys. The prime reason was to offer her some coaching on how to respond to them. The second was to spring a little surprise.

He stopped next to an oblong table in the space that did double duty as his personal office and conference room, and looked around. The offices of Patrick Sullivan, Esq., occupied the fourth floor of a converted five-story Lower East Side tenement; gray carpet, just this side of industrial grade, white walls and ceiling—the latter still sporting its original hammered tin which he'd decided he liked. His degrees and sundry official documents peppered the walls between indifferent prints he'd picked up from the Metropolitan Museum store. And of course he had his books and journals scattered on shelves and bookcases wherever there was room.

He heard the hall door open. Romy. He called out, "Back here!" but the woman who came through the door was not Romy.

"Mr. Sullivan?" said a thin, aging woman in a faded blue flowered dress and a rumpled red cardigan sweater. She wore a yellow scarf around her head, babushka style, and clutched a battered black handbag before her with both her bony hands. Her pale hazel eyes peered at him and she nodded vigorously. "Yes, you're him. I recognize you from the TV."

"Yes, ma'am?" he said. "Can I help you?"

She offered a smile that might have been girlish if she'd had more teeth. "I wish to retain your services, Mr. Sullivan."

The poor woman didn't look like she had enough for her next meal. But it could be a contingency case, and you never knew.

"In what regard, Ms . . . ?"

"Fredericks. *Miss* Alice Fredericks. And I want you to sue SimGen for me. I can tell you're a brave man. You were ready to take on the company on behalf of those poor dear sims, so I figure you're just the man, in fact the *only* man with the guts to tackle them for me."

"Do you? That's very gratifying. On what grounds do you wish me to tackle them, may I ask?"

Her face screwed up, accentuating her wrinkles, and looked as if she was about to cry. "They took my baby!" she wailed.

Baby? Patrick stared at her. A warning bell clanged in his brain. SimGen might be guilty of many things, but he doubted stealing babies was one of them. And this woman was long, long past the baby-bearing years.

"When did this happen?"

She sobbed. "Thirty years ago last month! The seventeenth, to be exact."

"That's quite a while, Miss Fredericks. Why have you waited so long to go after them?"

"I've been to every lawyer in the city and no one will take the case. They're all afraid!"

"I find that hard to believe, Miss Fredericks. There are literally thousands of lawyers in town who would get in line to sue SimGen."

"Sure . . . until they hear about the space aliens."

Oh, Christ. No need for a warning bell anymore. There it was, right out on the table for all to see: a big, multicolored bull's eye with "*Looney Tunes*" scrawled across it.

Patrick didn't want to ask but had to. "Aliens?"

"Yes. Space aliens abducted me, impregnated me, and then when I delivered, it was a sim. But I loved him anyway. That didn't matter, though. They took my baby boy away from me. And do you know who they handed him to? Right in front of me? Mercer Sinclair! Mercer Sinclair took my baby and I want him back!" She sobbed again.

She wasn't scamming. Patrick had a sensitive bullshit meter and it wasn't even twitching. This poor woman believed every word.

"I feel your pain, Miss Fredericks, but—"

"And you know what Mercer Sinclair did with my son, don't you? He made the whole race of sims from him. And he did it for the aliens so that earth can be repopulated by a slave race that the aliens can use around the galaxy."

Patrick blinked. A living breathing talking issue of *Weekly World News* had walked into his office. It might be funny if the woman weren't so genuinely upset. And he might be tempted to sit down and listen to her—purely for entertainment—if Romy weren't due momentarily.

"I'm afraid my schedule's rather full now, Miss Fredericks," he said. He glanced at his watch. "And I'm expecting a client for an important conference in just a few minutes and—"

"Oh, I'm so sorry. I should have made an appointment."

"That's okay." He pushed a legal pad and a pen across the table to her. "But I'll tell you what. Leave me your number and I'll call you when my schedule opens up."

"Then you're not afraid?" she said, scribbling on the sheet.

"Of SimGen? Never."

"I meant the space aliens. You're not afraid of the space aliens?"

"Never met one I couldn't take with one hand."

"Thank you," she said, puddling up again. "You don't know what this means to me."

"I'm sure I don't."

"That's the number of the phone in the hall outside my room. Just ask for me and someone will get me."

Patrick nodded. He felt a little bad, giving her the brush like this, but it was the gentlest way he knew to get her out of his office.

Romy entered as Alice was leaving.

"Who was that?"

"A poor soul with a crazy story about SimGen." Patrick shook his head. "If she's representative of my future clientele, I'm in big trouble. But never mind her." He spread his arms. "What do you think of my new office?"

"Not bad," she said, looking around as she seated herself at the mini conference table.

She was being generous, he knew. "I know what you're thinking, and I agree: I need a decorator."

"Not really." She smiled faintly as she gazed up at the patterned tin ceiling. "I kind of like the anti-establishment air of the place."

"So do I. Gives me a feeling of kinship with the likes of Darrow and Kuntsler."

She smiled. "Darrow, Kuntsler & Sullivan. What a firm."

"Better than my old firm, Nasty, Brutish, and Short."

He studied her across the table as she smiled. She looked good. The wicked shiners she'd developed after The Great Injury had faded from deep plum to sickly custard yellow. The sutures were gone from her scalp; she'd been able to hide the angry red seam by combing her short dark hair over it, but today she'd left it exposed for all the world to see.

"Want some coffee?" he said.

She shook her head. "I'm tense enough, thank you."

"How about decaffeinated? I can have my legal assistant perk up a pot in no time."

"Assistant? I didn't know you'd hired anyone."

"You don't expect a high-powered attorney like me to stoop to filing my own papers, do you?" Patrick turned toward the file room and called out, "Assistant! Oh, assistant! Can you come here a minute?"

Tome, who'd been waiting quietly and patiently behind the door as instructed, said, "Yes, Mist Sulliman."

Romy's eyes fairly bulged. "That sounds like—"

And then Tome, ever so dapper in his new white shirt, clip-on tie, and baggy blue suit, stepped into the room.

"It is!" she cried. She leaped to her feet and crossed the room in three long-legged strides. She threw her arms around Tome and hugged him as she looked at Patrick with wonder-filled eyes. "But how? You couldn't . . . you didn't . . ."

"Kidnap him? Not quite."

She kept an arm around the old sim as Patrick explained Tome's post-traumatic depression and the arrangement with Beacon Ridge. Because she was taller than Tome, Romy's bear hug pressed his head between her breasts.

Hey, that's where I should be, Patrick thought as Tome grinned at him.

Nothing salacious or suggestive in that smile, just pure happiness. Being away from the barracks had worked wonders on the old sim. Within two days he was up and about, eating with gusto. And once Patrick had taught him the rudiments of filing, Tome took to the task with religious zeal.

Romy barraged Tome with questions about how he was feeling and what he'd been doing since the tragedy. Patrick had things he needed to discuss with Romy so he gave them a little time to catch up, then interrupted.

"Tome, would you mind doing some more filing before our guests arrive?"

"Yes, Mist Sulliman."

After Tome disappeared into the file room, Romy turned to him. "Does he bunk here?"

"No. We're roomies."

"Roomies?" She gave her head a slow shake. "Am I hearing and seeing things? I've heard hallucinations can be an after-effect of head trauma."

"It's not so bad. He keeps pretty much to himself. I got him one of those compact TV-VCR combinations for his bedroom and he spends most of his time there."

Her eyes were bright as she stared at him. "What a wonderful, wonderful thing to do."

"He's a riot," Patrick said, grinning. "I bought him that suit and he's absolutely in love with it. I had to go out and buy an iron and a board because he insists on ironing it every night." She was still staring at him. "Hey, no biggee. I figure it's only for a month or so, till he gets back on his feet."

"Still, I never would have imagined . . ."

"I'm told I'm full of surprises." He pulled a packet of folded sheets from an inside pocket of his jacket and slid them across the table to Romy. "But I'm not the only one."

"What's this?"

"A report from the Medical Examiner's office on the three floaters from the Hudson."

"The globulin farmers? How'd you get it?"

"It arrived by messenger this morning, no return address, but I can guess."

Romy nodded. "So can I." They'd decided not to mention Zero by name if there was any chance of a bug nearby. "He has contacts everywhere."

"I can save you the trouble of reading it," Patrick said as she unfolded the pages. "Remember how the bodies showed signs of torture? Well, toxin analysis revealed traces of a synthetic alkaloid in the tissues of all three. I won't try to tell you the chemical name—it's in there and it's a mile long—but the report says it's known in the intelligence community as *totuus*; developed in Finland as a sort of 'truth' drug, and supposedly very effective."

"Totuus," Romy said, her face a shade paler. "I wonder if that's what they planned to use on me?"

"When?"

"When they drove us off the road. I remember one of them had a syringe and mentioned something about 'dosing' me up and getting a recorder ready."

She'd never told him. The news twisted his insides. "You think there's a connection between the SLA and—?"

"Who knows what was in that syringe? And even if it was this totuus stuff, it doesn't prove anything."

"I guess not. But listen to this: the report says the totuus was administered *before* they were tortured."

"I don't get it," Romy said. "Why use torture when you've got a truth drug?"

Patrick wandered to the window overlooking Henry Street and watched the traffic. The same question had been bothering him.

"Maybe for fun. I don't know what ideals are driving these SLA characters, but it's pretty clear now they're a vicious bunch."

"And if they want to 'free the sims' as they say, where are the ones they 'liberated'?"

"I was wondering the same thing. If they—"

A black Mercedes limo stopped and double parked on the street below. In this neighborhood that could mean only one thing.

"They're here," he said. "Fashionably early."

He watched as two dark-suited, briefcase-toting figures emerged, one male, one female; he noticed the woman lean back into the car and speak to someone still in the back seat.

Three arrive but only two come up. Odd . . .

"All right," he said, clapping his hands. "Places, everyone. Tome, you know what to do; Romy, you know your part. We've got only one shot at this so let's get it right."

The two Manassas Ventures attorneys arrived shortly, trying unsuccessfully to hide their astonishment at being welcomed by a sim. Introductions were made, cards exchanged. The woman, a redhead, thin and pale as a saltine, was Margaret Russo; the heavy, dark-haired man, who looked like he ate all his associate's leftovers, was David Redstone.

Russo glanced around. "Well, I must say, your office is . . . unique."

"And that elevator," Redstone said. "What an antique."

"It's steam powered," Patrick told them. "Can't be replaced because this is an historic building." He had no idea if any of that were true but it sounded good. "Shall we get started?"

He led them the short distance to the conference table where Romy waited. He made the introductions, then indicated chairs across the table from Romy for the Manassas people. He sat next to Romy.

"What's he doing?" Russo said, pointing to Tome who had situated himself on a chair behind and to Patrick's left with a steno pad propped on his lap.

"Taking notes," Patrick tossed off. "Now, before we—"

Russo was still staring. "But he's a sim. Sims can't write."

"It's shorthand. He'll type it up later."

He watched Russo and Redstone exchange glances. Good. Get them off balance and keep them there. They didn't need to know that Tome would be making meaningless scribbles or that Patrick was taping the meeting. He was sure they had their own tape recorders running.

"We'd like to get right down to business," Redstone said, pulling a legal pad from his briefcase. "The nitty gritty, as it were. To expedite matters I propose that we drop all pretense and skip the verbal jousting."

"No trenchant legal repartee?" Patrick said. "Where's the fun?"

"Look, Mr. Sullivan, we all know what this is about. We know Ms. Cadman was injured, but we also know the incident was set up."

Patrick glowered at her. "You'd better be able to back that up with facts, Ms. Russo."

"No jousting, remember?" she said. "Whatever it is you want, other than money, you're not going to get. So let's just end this charade here and now. We are authorized to make the following offer: Name a figure, any figure; tell us the magic number that will make you walk away from this, and we will pay it."

Patrick had been expecting an attempt to buy them off, but nothing this blatant. But if that was the way they wanted to play . . .

"A magic number," he said, tapping his chin and pretending to ponder the possibilities. "How does an even billion sound?"

Russo and Redstone blinked in unison.

Russo recovered first. She cleared her throat. "Are we going to have a serious discussion or not? Did you call us here to waste our time or—"

"Whoa," Patrick said. "First off, you called us. Secondly—let me check with my assistant here." He turned to Tome. "Didn't they say, 'Name a figure, any figure'?"

The sim consulted his steno pad and said, "Yes, Mist Sulliman."

Tome had been instructed to do just that, no matter what Patrick asked him.

"There, you see? 'Name any figure.' And I believe a billion is a figure."

"You can't possibly expect a small company like Manassas Ventures to come up with a sum like that," Russo said.

"Why not? It owns billions and billions worth of SimGen stock. But maybe it doesn't have the stock anymore. I've learned that it's a wholly owned subsidiary of MetaVentures, based in Atlanta, so maybe the stock went there. Or perhaps it traveled further up the ladder to MacroVentures, a Bahamian corporation. But MacroVentures is owned by MetroVentures in the Caymans. Maybe that's where the stock ended up. Wherever it is, we know one of these companies has the financial wherewithal to pay Ms. Cadman's 'magic number' in a heartbeat. So don't cry poverty to me."

"This is preposterous!" Redstone sputtered.

"Not as preposterous as you two trying to keep me from having my day in court," Romy said.

Patrick had instructed her to play it sincere, and she was doing fine, because she was genuinely outraged.

"Oh, please—" Russo began but Romy cut her off.

Here it comes, Patrick thought.

"All I wanted was a little information," Romy said. "Nothing complicated. I simply wanted someone to explain why a truck leased by Manassas Ventures in Idaho was driving around the SimGen campus in New Jersey."

He scrutinized the two attorneys, watching their reactions as Romy dropped her bomb.

He'd gone half crazy trying to ferret out the principals in all subsidiaries behind Manassas. Only the discovery proceedings of a lawsuit would give him a chance to pierce their multiple walls of secrecy. But it would still take him years to reach the end of the corporate shell game, and even then he might well come up empty. So he'd decided to shake things up by tossing a live snake into Manassas Ventures' corporate lap.

But neither Russo nor Redstone showed even a hint of surprise or concern. They were either clueless or had nervous systems of stone.

Damn.

"Write that down," Patrick said irritably, pointing to Redstone's legal pad. "It's important."

"What?"

"Your clients will want to know about those trucks. Trust me."

As Redstone made a note with a gold mechanical pencil, Russo said, "Can we stop playing games? A billion is out of the question."

"Out of the question?" Patrick said. "Gee. And we haven't even discussed punitive damages yet. I was thinking at least another billion—"

Russo slammed her hand on the table and shot to her feet. "That's it. I see no point in prolonging this farce. You two have an opportunity to be set for life. You've been offered the moon, but you want the stars."

"Very poetic."

She glared at him. "When you and your client come to your senses, Mr. Sullivan, call us."

"It won't be a call, it will be a subpoena. Many subpoenas. A blizzard of them. The first are already on their way."

"Send as many as you wish," Redstone said, snapping his briefcase closed. "You won't see a dime."

Patrick smiled. "Perhaps not, but we'll get what we want."

They stormed out.

After the door slammed, Romy said, "Wow. They're taking this personally."

"I've got a feeling they were offered a big bonus if they got the job done." He headed for the door. "Excuse me."

"Where are you going?" Romy said.

"Down to the street. I'll only be a minute."

He took the stairs and beat the Manassas attorneys to the lobby. He waited until they were outside, then trailed them to the limo. When they opened the door he caught up and leaned between them.

"You folks forgot to take my card, so I brought one down for each of you." He peered into the dim back seat and looked into the startled blue eyes of a balding man, easily in his seventies, sporting a dapper pencil-line mustache. "Hello," Patrick said. "Have we met? I'm—"

"Get in!" the man said to the two attorneys. He turned his head away from Patrick and spoke to the driver. "Go! We're through here!"

The doors slammed and the limo moved off.

Who's the old guy? Patrick wondered as he took the stairs back up to his office. He'd half-expected to see Mercer Sinclair or perhaps that Portero fellow, but he'd never seen this guy before. Whoever he was he hadn't seemed at all happy that Patrick had gotten a look at his face.

When he reached the office Romy was just finishing a call. She snapped the cell phone lid closed and turned to him.

"That was our mutual friend. I told him about the meeting and he's a little upset that we didn't clear your idea with him first."

"I'm not used to having a nanny," Patrick replied. "Besides, we're just stirring up the bottom of the pond to see what floats to the surface."

"He worried that mentioning the Manassas-Idaho truck connection at this point might give them time to cover their tracks. Or worse, precipitate a rash response."

"You mean like running my car off the road again? I don't think so."

Patrick didn't think whoever was behind Manassas would risk hurting him or Romy. That would raise too many questions; might even prompt a Grand Jury investigation into whether there was a connection.

"Still, he suggested that you invest in a remote starter for your car. Just in case."

Patrick stared at her, his mouth dry.

Romy smiled. "Joking."

Patrick was about to tell her where Zero could store his remote starter when her cell phone chirped again. He watched her face, expecting the usual light-up he'd noticed whenever she spoke to Zero, but instead her brow furrowed as she frowned.

"Have you got a car available?" she asked as she ended the call.

"I can get to it in about five minutes. Why?"

"Road trip." Her expression remained troubled.

"Something wrong"?

"One of my NYPD contacts. He gave me the address of a house in Brooklyn. Said they'd found something there that would interest me."

"He didn't say what?"

"No. He said I had to see it to believe it."

17

East New York

"One thing I've got to say about hanging with you," Patrick said as he drove them past peeling houses with littered yards. "I get to see all the city's ritziest neighborhoods. Say, you live in Brooklyn, don't you?"

Yes, Romy thought as she stared straight ahead through the windshield. She thought of the neat little shops and bistros along Court Street, just around the corner from her apartment in Cobble Hill. That was Brooklyn too, but a world away from this place. East New York was as far east as you could go in the borough. The economic boom of the nineties had run out of gas before it reached East New York. The faces were black, the cars along the trash-choked curbs old and battered, the mood grim.

"Hello?" Patrick said. "Are you still with me?"

She nodded and looked down at the map of Brooklyn unfolded on her lap. She knew she hadn't been good company on the slow, frustrating drive across the Manhattan Bridge and through the myriad neighborhoods of the borough, but the nearer they moved to their destination, the tighter the icy clamp around her stomach.

Lieutenant Milancewich's call nagged at her. Her tips had helped him make a few busts over the years and in return he occasionally gave her a heads-up on police investigations he thought might interest her. But he wasn't a friend, merely a contact, and she knew he considered her a little whacko. Maybe a lot whacko. He had no use for sims and thought her a bit overzealous in her one-woman war against sim abusers, but a bust was a bust and he was glad to have credit for them on his record.

Today, though, she'd heard something strange in his voice; she couldn't identify it, but knew she'd never heard it before. She'd pressed him about what it was he wanted her to see but he wouldn't say anything beyond, *I ain't been there myself, so I don't want to pass on any secondhand reports, but if what I hear is true, you should be there.*

Is it bad? she'd asked.

It ain't good.

And that was what bothered her. The strange note in his voice when he'd said, *It ain't good.*

"I hope we're almost there," Patrick said. "I don't think I want to get lost out here, especially with sundown on the way."

She focused on the map. "Make a left up here onto—there!" She pointed to a pair of blue-and-white units just around the corner. "See the lights?"

"Got 'em."

Patrick pulled into the curb and they both stepped out. He led the way as they wound through the thin crowd clustered outside the yellow crime scene tape. Once they were past the tape, Romy took the lead. Three of the four cops at the scene were either in their units or leaning against them as they talked on two-ways. Romy approached the fourth, a patrolman sipping a cup of coffee outside the front door of a shabby, sagging Cape Cod. He looked to be in his late twenties, fair skinned, with a reddish-blond mustache.

After showing him her ID and going through the what-is-OPRR? and what's-OPRR-got-to-do-with-this? explanations, and making sure to smile a lot, she got him to open up.

"Got a call about a bad smell coming from the place." He cocked his head toward the house as he spoke in an accent that left no doubt he was a native of the borough. "So we investigated. Had to kick in the front door and that's when it really hit us. Ain't the first time I smelled that."

"Somebody dead?"

"That's what we figured, only we had it wrong. Not *some*body—*many* bodies. And they ain't human."

Romy closed her eyes and took a deep breath. She was afraid to ask. "How many?"

"Looks like a dozen."

She heard Patrick's sharp intake of breath close behind her.

"How many sims were taken from the globulin farm?" he asked.

"Thirteen," she said without turning. "At least they think it housed thirteen." That was the count the police had painstakingly gleaned from one of the hard drives plucked from the ashes.

"Hey, you think these might be the missing sims from that Bronx fire last week?" The cop shook his head. "Don't that beat all. I thought that job was pulled by a bunch of sim lovers."

"These may have no relation."

How could they? It didn't make sense that people who spray-painted "Death to sim oppressors" would kill the very sims they'd liberated.

The cop said, "Well, if they're the same, I'd guess from the stink and the condition of the bodies that they were done the same night as the fire." He shook his head in disgust. "Pisses me off."

Surprised, Romy looked at him. "Killing sims?"

"You kidding? No way. I mean, I'm not in favor of someone going around killing dumb animals, but what pisses me is that even though they ain't human I gotta hang around with my thumb up my ass—'scuse the French, okay?— while everybody figures out what to do and who should do it."

"How'd they die?" Romy asked.

"Don't need no forensics team for that." He poked his index finger against his temple and cocked his thumb. "Bam! One to the head for each of them. Must've used jacketed slugs because—"

"Thank you," Romy said, holding up a hand.

"Yeah, well, it was messy, all right. But not near as messy as what was done to them after they was shot."

Romy stiffened. "What do you mean?"

"Sliced them open from here"—his gun barrel finger became a scalpel and he dragged it from the base of his throat to his groin—"to here."

"Christ!" Patrick said.

Romy swallowed back a surge of bile. "Why on earth . . .?"

"Beats me. Dragged all their guts out and piled them in the middle of the cellar floor. Freaking mess down there, and if they think I'm gonna clean it up because it's 'evidence,' they can—"

"I want to see," Romy said.

"No, you don't, lady. If there's one thing I know in this life, lady, it's you do not want to go down in that cellar."

He's absolutely right, Romy thought. I don't.

But she had to see this for herself. Nothing made sense. If these were the sims from the globulin farm, what were they doing here? Had they been "liberated" just to be executed and mutilated?

Setting her jaw to keep her composure, Romy pulled a stick of gum—Starburst Cinnamon—from her purse and began to chew.

The cop nodded knowingly. "I see you've been down this street before."

"What's going on?" Patrick said.

She turned and offered him a stick, saying, "Because sometimes the smell's so thick you can taste it."

"You're going in?" he said. He looked genuinely concerned. "That's way above and beyond, Romy. Leave it for the forensics people. You don't have to do this."

"Yeah, I do," she said. "Because they're sims the M-E will give them a cursory once-over, if that. Most likely the remains will be shipped back to SimGen and we'll never hear a thing. I don't expect you to come with me, Patrick. In fact, I'd prefer you didn't. But I need to see what's been done, so I can get a feel for the kind of monsters we're dealing with here."

She turned to the patrolman. "Let's go."

"Sorry," he said, shaking his head. "Might smell a little better in there now with the doors open, but I'm not going back in until I have to." He pointed toward the open front door. "Once you're inside, head straight back to the kitchen; hang a U and you'll be facing the cellar stairs." He handed her his flashlight. "There's no electricity so you'll need this. Just don't drop it. Or blow lunch on it."

"Thanks. I won't."

Knowing that if she hesitated she might lose her nerve, Romy immediately put herself in motion. She'd examined dead sims before, some of them in a ripe state of decomposition, and had learned some tricks along the way.

She'd gained the top of the two crumbling front steps and was pulling a tissue from her purse when she sensed someone behind her.

Patrick. His face looked pale, and despite the cold she thought she detected a faint sheen of sweat across his forehead.

"Wait for me out here," she told him.

"Sorry, no. I could have stayed in the yard if the cop had gone with you, but I can't let you go down there alone."

"Patrick—"

"Let's not argue about it, okay. I'm going in. Give me a stick of that gum and we'll get this over with."

She stared at him a moment. Patrick Sullivan was turning out to be a gutsy guy. She handed him a tissue along with the gum.

"When we head down to the cellar, hold this over your mouth and nose, pinching the nostrils and breathing into the tissue. That way you'll rebreathe some of your own air."

He nodded, his expression grim as he unwrapped the gum and stuck it into his mouth. "Let's go."

Romy led the way. Despite the open doors front and rear, the odor was still strong on the main floor; but when she rounded the turn and stood before the doorless opening leading down from the kitchen, it all but overpowered her. She heard Patrick groan behind her.

"Tissue time," she said. "And it could be worse. At least it's winter and the cold slows down decomposition. Imagine if this were August."

Patrick made no reply. Romy stared at the dark opening of the cellar doorway. She wished there were someone else she could unload this on, but couldn't think of a soul.

Steeling herself, she flicked on the flashlight and started down into the blackness. She kept the beam on the steps, moving carefully because there was no railing. The odor was indescribable. It made her eyes water, and even with her nostrils pinched, it wormed its way around the cinnamon gum in her mouth and made a rear entry to her nasal passages by seeping up past her soft palate.

When she reached the bottom Romy angled the beam ahead, moving it across the concrete. At first she thought someone had started painting the floor black and run out of paint three-quarters of the way through; then she realized it was blood. Old, dried blood. The cellar must have been awash in it.

She flicked the beam left and right to get her bearings and stopped when it lit up what looked like a pile of dirty rope. She remembered what the cop had said—*dragged all their guts out and piled them in the middle of the cellar floor*—and knew she wasn't looking at rope.

She swallowed back a surge of bile and forced herself forward, trying not to step in the dried blood—might be evidence there—as she moved. She stopped again when her beam reflected off staring eyes and bared teeth. She'd found the dead sims. Clad only in caked blood, their bodies ripped from stem to stern, they'd been stacked like cordwood against one of the walls. Their dead eyes and slack mouths seemed to be asking, *Why? Why?* And she wanted to scream that she didn't know.

Behind her she heard Patrick retch. She turned and saw him leaning against one of the support columns.

"You okay?" she said through her tissue.

"No." His voice was hoarse. He held up a thumb and forefinger; they appeared to be touching. "I'm just this far away from losing my lunch."

"I skipped lunch, thank God." She paused, then, "Look, I need to get closer."

"I don't. I'll stay back here and guard the steps, if you don't mind."

"I appreciate it," she told him. He'd already proved himself as far as she was concerned.

Turning, she spotted fresh, dusty prints ahead in the dried blood, leading to the cadavers; one of the cops, no

doubt. To avoid further contamination of the scene she used them as stepping stones to move forward, knowing all along that it was wasted effort—no one was going to spend much time sifting this abattoir for clues. But there was a right way to do something, and then there was every other way.

Closer now she flashed her beam into the gaping incision running the length of the nearest cadaver's naked torso. A female. Her ribs had been ripped back, revealing lungs but no heart. Romy leaned forward and checked the abdominal cavity. Liver and kidneys gone. She craned her neck to see into the pelvis—uterus and ovaries missing too.

She moved onto another, a male this time, and the results were similar except that his testicles had been removed.

Romy straightened. They'd been gutted, all of them, and the males castrated. She took a quick turn around the rest of the basement but found no sign of the excised organs. The intestines had been removed and discarded in a pile because they were valueless and only got in the way. But all the rest were missing.

"Let's go," Romy said, taking Patrick's arm and pointing up the steps toward daylight and fresher air. "I've seen enough."

More than enough.

They hurried to the first floor and back out to the front yard. Romy didn't understand the missing ovaries and testicles—she knew of no use for them—but she understood the rest all too well.

Furious, she went straight to the cop and slapped the flashlight back into his palm.

"Didn't you notice anything missing down there?" she said.

He looked uncomfortable. "Like what?"

"Like their organs! They weren't just killed, they were harvested! And *that*"—she jabbed a finger at his chest—"is a felony!"

18

Harlem

Beece work ver hard today. Many cloth to cut. Boss say, Faster, faster! Beece cut fast as can. Still boss yell.

Beece ver hot. Thirsty. Go sink for drink. Drink quick 'cause sink next boss office. Too long drink boss yell.

Boss door open. New man walk through. Red-hair man. Show boss papers. Beece hear talk.

"I'm from the city Animal Control Center, Mr. Lachter."

"Hey, I treat my sims good."

"No, Mr. Lachter, that would fall under the auspices of the ASPCA. We have a different mandate, and at the moment we're looking for a lost sim."

Beece almost leave sink, now stay. Lost sim? Could be Meerm? Listen more.

"I got all mine. I count 'em every morning. None missing, no extras."

"Good. But from past experience we know that lost sims tend to seek out other sims, so we'd greatly appreciate it if you'd keep your eye out for any sim that might wander in."

Boss laugh. "He does, I'll put him to work!"

"It's a female and if she shows up you should isolate her immediately."

"Why's that?"

"She may be sick. Nothing contagious to humans, but she might infect other sims."

Infect? Beece think. What mean infect?

"I don't need none of that. I can barely make production quotas now."

"If she shows she may look a little different than the average sim and—"

"Different? What is she, a new breed?"

"No. Same as the rest, but she might look a little heavier . . . perhaps 'bloated' is a better term. She's sick and we can take care of her, but we have to find her first."

Meerm! Man talk about Meerm! Meerm sick but fraid doctor. Beece feel sorry Meerm. City Man want help Meerm. No hurt Meerm.

Beece fraid talk Boss. Boss yell all time. But Meerm Beece friend. Must help Meerm.

Beece step in office. " 'Scuse, please, boss."

Boss face go mad. "What the hell you doing here! Get back to work, you lazy—"

"No, wait," red-hair city man say. He look Beece. "Do you know something?"

"Sick sim come home."

"Home? Where's home?"

"I crib them in Newark overnight," Boss say.

"Newark? Why so far?"

"Because it's tons cheaper to bus them back and forth than rent space for them around here. Sorry if that's out of your jurisdiction, pal, but—"

"Oh, don't you worry about that. Just give me the address of this place. I'll take it from there."

Beece happy. Red-hair city man nice. Help Meerm. Make Meerm better.

19

Sussex County, NJ

"This is good," Mercer Sinclair said as he skimmed the reports. "This is very good."

Just SimGen's security chief in the office with him today. Portero had personally delivered the police reports on the sim massacre in Brooklyn, an unusual courtesy. Perhaps the man was coming around, learning to be a team player.

Who am I kidding? Someone like Harry Carstairs is a team player, but not Luca Portero. He doesn't know the meaning of the word "team." He smiled to himself. Come to think of it, neither do I.

This visit meant one thing: Portero wanted something.

He'd never come right out and ask, Mercer knew. He'd use an oblique approach, try to sneak it in when no one was looking. Mercer was sure he'd find out what it was before the meeting ended.

"I thought you'd be upset," Portero said.

Is that why he came? To watch me blow my top? Sorry, Little Luca. Not today.

"I am. I hate the idea of losing a dozen of our sims. That's something people seem to forget—they're *our* sims. No matter what country they're shipped to, even if it's the other side of the world, they still belong to SimGen. We can barely keep up with demand as it is, so of course I hate to lose even one sim."

"But you seem almost . . . happy."

"I'm happy that these SLA creeps have been exposed for what they are: they're not pro-sim activists, they're murderous organleggers." He glanced at the police report again. "They're sure these are the same sims that were hijacked from the globulin farm?"

Portero nodded. "Absolutely. Lucky thing NYPD was able to resuscitate that hard drive from the ashes in the Bronx. And lucky too these globulin farmers were excellent record keepers: they scanned the neck bar codes of all their 'cows' into their computers."

"Then that nails the SLA. When they're caught they'll go down for murder and illegal organ trafficking. Any chance of tracing those organs?"

Portero shrugged. "Unlikely. They were probably shipped overseas immediately. I've heard the Third World black market for transplant organs is really booming, but . . ." He looked troubled.

"But what?"

"I know there's a big demand for human organs, but sim organs?"

"They're called xenografts—non-human organs. Human bodies used to reject them almost immediately, but with the new treatments that remove histo-compatibility antigens, the rejection rate is about equal to human allografts. Those hearts, livers and kidneys are worth a fortune on the black market."

Portero nodded and Mercer thought, You haven't a clue as to anything I just said. Went right over your head.

"Hearts, livers, kidneys," Portero said. "What about uteruses and ovaries? Are they transplantable?"

"No value at all. Nor are the testicles they cut off—unless someone's developed a taste for a new kind of Rocky Mountain oyster."

Just the thought made Mercer ill.

"Then why go to the trouble to harvest them?"

"Maybe they were stupid organleggers."

"One other thing concerns me," Portero said. "The hard drive from the globulin farm shows records of thirteen sims housed there right up until the night of the fire. But only twelve were found in that Brooklyn basement. I rechecked the reports from the Bronx fire and no sim remains were found in the ashes.

"You're sure?"

"Absolutely."

"You think he might have escaped?"

"She. We know from the records that a female sim is unaccounted for. According to the records, the only bar code unaccounted for belongs to a twelve-year old named Meerm. And the only reason I can imagine why she wasn't butchered along with the rest is that she wasn't with them."

"You think she escaped?"

"I suspect she was never captured. I think she fled the raid and the fire, and is hiding somewhere in the city."

"Why on earth would she hide?"

"Maybe she saw the security man murdered and she's frightened. She could be anywhere, too terrified to show herself."

A witness, Mercer thought. A sim could never testify in court, but this one might be able to provide the police with a lead or two.

Mercer glanced down at the embedded monitor in his desktop. Damn near every headline scrolling up the screen this morning seemed to be about the sim slaughter in Brooklyn. The good part was that the phony "SLA" had shown its true colors; the bad part was the depiction of sims as helpless victims, easy prey for human scum. Too high a sympathy factor there. He needed to counter that, and this missing sim offered a unique opportunity.

"I want that sim found," he told Portero. "To make sure she is, SimGen is going to offer a million-dollar reward to whoever finds her."

Portero looked dubious. "Do you think that's necessary? I'm sure my people—"

"Forget your people. This is strictly a SimGen matter. We'll handle it."

Yes. The more he thought about this, the more he liked it. Here was a way to take back the headlines and reassert SimGen as the true champion and defender of sims.

"Very well," Portero said, rising. "Since there's nothing for me to do in that regard, I'll get back to my office."

After Portero was gone it occurred to Mercer that he hadn't discovered the reason for the security chief's personal visit. He'd been sure he'd wanted something. But what?

Well, whatever it was, he hadn't got it.

20

Luca Portero went directly from Sinclair-1's office to the parking lot where he picked up one of the SimGen Cherokees and drove out the gate. The meeting had gone just as he'd hoped, and he'd be laughing now if not for what lay ahead. Another meeting. This one with Darryl Lister. He and his superior hadn't had a face-to-face meeting in almost a year, which could only mean that the subject was as delicate as it was important.

Worse yet, they were meeting at Luca's house.

He pulled up the long drive to the rented two-bedroom ranch in the center of five acres of dense woods. He liked the isolation. This was his retreat from the pressure cooker his daily life had become.

Damn. Lister had beat him here. At least Luca assumed the black Mercedes SUV belonged to Lister. Was he alone? With the late morning sun glinting off the SUV's windshield, Luca couldn't tell how many were in the car.

When he pulled up next to it he was startled to see that it was empty. He hurried to his front door—unlocked. He stepped through and found Darryl Lister waiting inside.

Lister was in his late forties; the brown corduroys and bulky white Irish wool sweater he wore couldn't hide the inches he'd added to his waist since Luca had last seen him. And judging from the new gelled-up hairstyle, it looked like he'd started going to a fag barber.

He smirked at Luca. "Where'd you furnish this place, Portero? Secondhand stores?"

Luca felt invaded. He wanted to scream at Lister to get out of his fucking house, but bit it back. He gently closed the door behind him. Didn't want to make a fuss. Might give Lister the idea that he had something to hide. Didn't want to do that.

"It came with the territory. It's a furnished rental."

"You rent? I'm sure we pay you enough so you can afford to buy."

Luca wanted to punch him. Lister knew exactly what he made, and must have known he rented. Why the charade?

As for renting, Luca saw no point in tying up money in real estate. He wanted no anchors. When the time came to move on, as it inevitably would, he wanted to be able to pick up and go without a second's hesitation, without a single look back.

"Glad you made yourself at home," Luca said. "Can I get you anything?"

Cyanide? Rat poison?

"No. I haven't got much time and there is an urgent matter we must discuss."

"If it's about the missing sim, I just enlisted Mercer Sinclair's help—a million-dollar reward—and he thinks it was his idea. Doesn't have a clue that I steered him into the whole thing."

The meeting had been a thing of beauty, he had to admit. Knowing Sinclair-1's obsession with SimGen's public image, Luca had simply parceled out the information—first playing dumb about the xenografts, then mentioning an unaccounted-for sim, then hinting that she might be a witness—letting Sinclair pounce from one to the next like a mouse following a trail of bits of cheese, until he'd ended up right where Luca wanted him.

A reward! Put SimGen in the news: The corporation with a heart as big as its market cap value!

Putty in my hands, Luca thought.

Lister was looking at him. "You haven't told the Sinclairs yet?"

"Not till I find the sim. I've got people combing the city, visiting any place that uses sim labor. This reward will flush out someone who's seen her. Once I have her, the Sinclairs can take over."

Lister frowned. "You might have had this sewn up by now if they'd been on board from the start."

"They'd have added nothing but panic." Bad enough to have Lister calling twice a day, he didn't need the Sinclairs yammering in his ear every free minute too. "And don't forget, it took days for the fire department to sift through all the rubble. Until they reported no sim remains, we didn't know for sure she was missing."

"Still, if this million-dollar reward had been announced days ago . . ."

Why didn't the bastard let it go? "You know my problem with telling SimGen too much."

"This 'leak' you suspect?"

Luca nodded.

Lister shoved his hands in his pockets and looked around. "I thought you were way off base with that at first," he said. "Now I'm not so sure."

"Why? What's happened?"

"The Manassas attorneys met with the Cadman woman and Sullivan. What a farce. She could have walked away with millions but she's asking for *billions* in damages."

Luca wanted to laugh. He'd known they couldn't buy her off. "Did you agree to pay it?"

Lister stared at him. "You're not serious."

"You should have called their bluff, just to see what they'd do. Because we all know they're not after money. But what does this have to do with a leak?"

"The Cadman woman said she'd come to the Manassas office because she wanted to know why a truck leased in Idaho by Manassas was driving around the SimGen campus."

"But . . ." Luca's heart stalled, then picked up again. "But there is no connection. Those leases are paid through Golden's credit card."

Hal Golden was dead, but no one knew that. His body lay six feet deep in a field in Thailand, but his credit record lived on, active and pristine, in the computers of the finance world. Golden had never even heard of Manassas Ventures while he lived, so how had Cadman and Sullivan linked him to the company?

"I know that. But at one time Manassas leased them directly. Somehow she made the connection. And I'm beginning to wonder if she might have been tipped."

"But that doesn't make sense. If someone's leaking her information about Manassas Ventures, wouldn't they tell her everything?"

"You'd think so, wouldn't you. But whatever her source, somehow this woman has identified Manassas as the tie between SimGen and our Idaho facility."

"So then, why not just abandon Manassas? It served its purpose."

"It's not like some dinghy you can cut loose at sea and forget. It's part of a chain of subsidiary corporate entities that this Sullivan fuck has already traced back four or five levels. This has *everyone* upset."

The way Lister emphasized "everyone" made it clear to Luca that this went far up the ladder.

"We want the woman and the lawyer stopped," Lister added, staring at him.

Me? Oh, no. "I'd love to help but I'm a little busy right now trying to find that sim. So why doesn't—"

"You were in charge of the Cadman woman when she saw the truck with the Idaho plates. That puts responsibility square in your lap, Portero. Take care of it."

"What? Take her out? If anything happens to her, anything *final*, Manassas Ventures will be a prime suspect."

Lister's voice dripped with contempt. "I'm talking about *information*, not termination. She's obviously not alone in this. We want to know who's behind her. We want her source. And if there's a leak in SimGen, we want to know who it is. Word has come down: this has equal priority with the missing sim. Understand, Portero? This isn't me talking to you. This comes from the Old Man himself."

The Old Man? Luca swallowed. That meant this went *all* the way up the ladder, and all eyes would be upon him. Damn Lister for laying this on him. And double damn Romy Cadman for mentioning that truck. It almost seemed like she was doing everything in her power to screw him.

"Don't look so put-upon," Lister said. "If you'd done the job right the first time, when you rolled Sullivan's car off the Saw Mill, we wouldn't be facing this problem now. You should be grateful for an opportunity to redeem yourself for that screw up."

"I am." He had to force the two words past stiff lips.

Luca felt the pressure growing within his head. Someone was out to get him. That was what this was about. Dump more on him than any one man could handle, then wait for him to buckle under the weight.

"Of course, if you feel you're overburdened and it's too much to handle—"

Luca's cell phone chirped. He flipped it open and turned away from Lister as he spoke. "Yes."

"This is Grimes. We found her. She's been hiding out in a sim crib."

Relief flooded through him. "You have her?"

"Not yet. But we've got an address and we're on our way."

"Where's the crib?" Luca listened as Grimes read off a Newark address. "I'll meet you there."

He ended the call and turned back to Lister. "One of my men. We've located the missing sim. We're on our way to pick her up." He grinned at Lister. "Overburdened? Lay it on me. I thrive on this stuff."

"We'll see," Lister said.

Bastard. Luca headed for the door. "You'll have to let yourself out. I've got work to do."

Newark. Not a long drive. And the timing could not be better. Tying this up would free him up to devote all his energies toward dealing with Romy Cadman, and settling accounts with her once and for all.

21

Newark

Meerm lonely. Not hungry. Nibble food save from last night. Watch out window. See peoples walk sidewalk. Not far down. One floor. Meerm listen. Sometime hear what passing peoples say. Sometime happy. Sometime mad. Meerm like happy better.

Meerm watch street. Many car but no sim bus. Wait sim bus. Hope come soon. Then friend Beece come. Belly pain hurt less when Beece near. Beece talk Meerm, help Meerm.

Meerm see car come fast. Stop outside. Four sunglass mans come. Look round, look sim building. Meerm quick step back. Who mans? Why here? Why look at sim building?

Meerm fraid mans come in. Peek so mans not see. No mans come in. All stand by car. One talk little phone. Why here?

Then Meerm see new car. Also fast. Stop next first car. One man come. New man talk loud. Point this way and that way. Other mans go. New man voice . . . Meerm hear before. But where?

Now Meerm see new man and other man come sim building. Meerm fraid. Mans come take Meerm away? Back to bad place where mans hurt Meerm?

Meerm hide. Go closet. Push self into dark corner. Make ver small.

Hear yell downstair. Benny mad. Shout loud. New man yell back.

Meerm shake. Know new man voice! Same voice in old home night loud noise and fire. Hear on roof too. New man come get Meerm!

Hear loud feets on stairs. Must not find! Must not find! Meerm climb up in closet. Get on shelf. Curl up. Make small-small. Tiny-tiny-tiny. Push back into high corner and—

Corner move. Meerm turn, feel loose board. Meerm push board, move more. Black space open. Cold in hole. Meerm not care. Too fraid be cold.

Hear new man voice yell, "Damn it, where is she?" Voice close now. In sim sleep room.

Meerm squeeze into black hole. Ooh-ooh-ooh. Too tight. Meerm so fat now. Meerm fraid get stuck, but more fraid new man. Push-push-push, get fat self into hole.

"I tell you," Benny say, "we ain't got no sims here inna day!" Benny sound fraid. "Not till tonight when they all bussed back from the city."

"She's here!" new man say. "And we're going to find her! Look under every bunk! Check every closet!"

Meerm in cold place inside wall. Ver tight. Ver dark. Meerm push on board, push back where belong. More dark now. All dark.

Meerm hear closet door squeak. Some man open. Meerm can't see man but hear thing move. Meerm stay ver, ver still. Not breathe.

"Nothing in here." New man voice ver close. Meerm so fraid. Want go pee. Bite lip stop cry. "Where the fuck *is* she?"

"Maybe she goes out," say other man voice. "You know, walks around."

"Since when did you became a sim expert?"

Other man say, "Hey, I'm just thinking out loud, okay? That sim at the sweatshop described her to a T: she's lost, she's sick, she's blown up. So we know she's staying here. She's just not here now. Probably going stir crazy here alone all day."

"All right. Here's what we'll do. Bring in the others and we'll do a sweep of the building. If we don't find her we'll back off and put the place under twenty-four-hour watch. When she returns, we nab her."

Meerm hear mans go way but still not move. Still fraid. Meerm must stay in sim building. Mans will get Meerm. Hurt Meerm if try leave. Meerm so sad she cry.

22

Sussex County, NJ

Luca wanted to skip this—he had far more pressing things to do than listen to Sinclair-1 yammer. But the man had said he was calling this late meeting specifically to address security issues, so Luca could hardly back out of that.

But he didn't have to arrive on time. He was punctual by nature, and his years in Special Forces had reinforced that, so it took considerable mental effort to force himself to walk slowly down the hall, pacing himself to arrive at least three minutes late.

Luca balled his fists. Coming up empty in the sim crib this afternoon still rankled him. Fury and disappointment had mixed into a combustible compound in his bloodstream. His head felt like a ticking bomb. He'd left four men to watch the building—all sides, all day, all night—but he had a gnawing premonition that the missing sim wouldn't be back.

Then, just fifteen minutes ago, Lister calls, supposedly concerned about the well-being of the sim because he hadn't heard any word on her. Luca had had to eat some bitter crow.

As if that wasn't bad enough, Lister then proceeded to twist the knife: "Someone handed you the address where she was staying and she ducked you? If a monkey can outwit you, how can we expect you to find out who's behind the woman and her lawyer?"

Don't worry, Luca thought as he approached the door to Sinclair-1's office. She's next on my list. And I know just how to handle her. The wheels go into motion as soon as I finish with these assholes.

When he stepped into the office he found only two of the usual crew in attendance: Sinclair-1, Sinclair-2 were present, but Abel Voss was missing.

"Mr. Portero," Sinclair-1 said as soon as the door closed. "We've been waiting for you."

"The wait is over," Luca replied. He wanted to get this meeting, at least his part of it, over with as quickly as possible, so he pushed right to the subject, "You mentioned a security matter?"

"Yes, Mr. Portero. Were you aware that we had an attempted break-in this afternoon?"

"Of course." A group of sim huggers had tried to run the front gate. His men detained them at the gate until the State Police arrived. "They're in jail."

"How gratifying that you know. But my question is, Where were you?"

"Busy with other matters."

"What other matters, pray tell? Matters more important than the security of the SimGen campus?

Security here is your responsibility, Mr. Portero. It is your number one priority. There are murderous bioterrorists running around out there, slaughtering humans and sims, and yet when this group tried to invade the campus, you were nowhere to be found."

"Harmless nobodies," Luca said, allowing a sneer to work its way onto his face. What an old woman he was.

"Lucky for us. But with you hiding out somewhere, there's no telling what damage we might have suffered if they'd been the SLA."

A flash of anger added heat to the pressure pushing against his eardrums. Hiding? Had this pantywaist of an empty suit just accused him of hiding?

"Easy, Mercer," said Sinclair-2, turning his head to look at Luca. This was the first sign of life he'd shown since Luca had arrived.

With difficulty Luca kept his voice level. "But they weren't the SLA."

"But they could have been!" Sinclair-1 said. He pointed over his shoulder at the darkening hills visible through the oversized picture window behind him. "The SLA could be out there now in the trees, readying an assault."

"They're not, and they never will be." Luca had had just about enough of playing games with these two. "I guarantee it."

Sinclair-1's eyebrows rose halfway to his forehead. "You guarantee it? How interesting. You're clairvoyant?"

"No," he gritted. "I'm the SLA."

Immediately he wished he hadn't said it.

"This is no time for sick humor," Sinclair-1 said.

Luca knew from the dubious expression on the CEO's face that he had a chance to take it back, but decided against it. Fuck 'em. He stepped up to Sinclair-1's desk, rested his hands on its cool onyx surface, and leaned forward, literally getting in the other man's face.

"That was not any kind of humor."

"What?" The voice from his right, Sinclair-2, on his feet, his face pale. "You?"

"Ellis, he's joking."

Luca fixed Sinclair-1 with his gaze. "Have you *ever* known me to joke?"

The CEO wavered, then took a step back, his eyes wide.

Movement to Luca's right. "Monster!" Sinclair-2 charging, face distorted with fury. Luca pivoted, drove a fist into his gut, and that was all she wrote. The man doubled over, then dropped to his knees, gasping for air.

"Dear, God! Ellis! Are you all right?"

The kneeling man, still clutching his belly with one hand while the other clutched the arm of the sofa for support, shook his head. His voice was a half-strangled whisper. "I'll never be all right."

Sinclair-1 stared at Luca. "Why? In God's name, *why?*"

"To find a particular sim."

"For what?" Sinclair-2 said as he hauled himself back into the couch. He sat hunched over, rubbing his belly. "To harvest her organs along with the rest?"

"No. To give her to you two."

"Why would we be interested?"

"Because she's pregnant."

A pause as the two brothers glanced at each other, then stared at Luca.

Sinclair-1 snorted. "Impossible!"

"So I've been told." Luca shrugged. "And maybe that's true in theory. But I deal in facts, and everything I've discovered about this particular sim confirms that she is pregnant."

"How on earth did you find out about her?"

Might as well tell them the whole story, Luca thought. Well, most of it. Can't tell them everything.

"It started with a phone call a few weeks ago. A woman said she had to speak to Mercer Sinclair right away, said she had information that would affect the entire future of SimGen. That sounded like a security matter to me so I took the call and—"

"And pretended to be me?"

"Of course. The woman, whose name I later learned was Eleanor Bryce, a Ph.D. in microbiology, told me she was in possession of a pregnant sim."

"You accepted that?" Sinclair-2 said. "Just like that?"

His color was returning along with his voice, but pure hatred gleamed in his eyes.

Portero returned his stare. You want another try for a piece of me, fancy man? Next time I spread your nose across your face.

"Of course not. In an involved back-and-forth that took days she sent enough information to convince our people that she could be telling the truth."

"*Your* people!" Sinclair-1 now. "The ones in our basic research facility, I suppose. Why not ours?"

"We were going to bring in your people later, but first we had to secure this sim. The Bryce woman made enough slips during our communications to allow me to pinpoint her location. When she presented her ultimatum I decided it was time to move."

"What was her ultimatum?" Sinclair-1 said.

That's not what you should be asking me, Luca thought. Why aren't either of you asking the right question?

Because he was dying to lay the answer on them . . . and watch both the Sinclair brothers' hair turn white before his eyes.

Luca said, "She wanted to sell us the sim."

"*Sell* us? Sell us something that already belonged to us? What did you tell her?"

"Since I was pretending to be you, I said exactly that, then I asked her how much she wanted. She told me to bid. And she warned me not to be 'chintzy'—her word—because there'd be another bidder: the Arata-jinruien Corporation."

Sinclair-1 pounded a fist on his desktop. "*Those* bandits? Outrageous!"

"Wait just a minute," Sinclair-2 said, holding up a hand. "Let's take a step back here."

Here it comes, Luca thought. His gut tingled with anticipation.

"Let's just say," Sinclair-2 continued, but he spoke to his brother, as if Luca weren't there, "that this Bryce woman, through hormone treatments or a recombinant patch, did somehow manage to induce a female sim to produce a fertilizable ovum. That will cause SimGen problems because it means people will be able to breed their own sims—and no one on this planet wants that less than I do—but it doesn't invalidate our patent on the sim genome. So—"

Not the question!

"She didn't do anything to the sim," Luca snapped. "She's a microbiologist. Knows nothing about reproductive medicine."

"How can you be sure?" Sinclair-1 said.

"She told me."

Sinclair-1 barked a laugh.

Luca glared at him. "At the time I questioned her she was loaded up with a drug that made her incapable of lying."

"The compound mentioned in the autopsy report," Sinclair-2 said, his tone dripping contempt. "Did you torture them before or after you had your information?"

"That was just window dressing, to muddy the waters while I eliminated everyone with firsthand knowledge about the pregnancy. I didn't know what the sims knew, but I didn't want any loose ends, so they were removed too."

"Dear God, why?" Sinclair-2 said. "A pregnant sim opens up a can of worms, but it's not worth the lives of four people and a dozen sims!"

Here's the moment, Luca thought. Time to rock your world.

"It does if the father of the sim's baby is human."

Silence, a moment of glorious, absolute silence in the office as the Sinclair brothers froze. Luca could have been looking at a photograph, or an elaborate sculpture. Then the thump of Sinclair-1 dropping heavily into his chair as if the bones in his legs had suddenly dissolved.

Luca inhaled the mixture of shock and terror filling the air. Moments like this made life worth living.